TO Camilla

Valberg

With my
Best Wishes

DESMOND
J. DOHERTY

Desmond J. Doherty

GUILDHALL PRESS

ISBN: 978 1 906271 74 9

Copyright © Desmond J. Doherty/Guildhall Press 2013

Author's photo (inside front cover) © Mustafa Oymak

Scaffolding taken from *Death of a Naturalist* © Seamus Heaney and reprinted by kind permission of Faber and Faber Ltd.

The author asserts his moral rights in this work in accordance with the Copyright, Designs and Patents Act 1998.

First published June 2013, reprinted October 2013

Guildhall Press
Ráth Mór Business Park
Bligh's Lane, Derry
Ireland
BT48 0LZ
00 44 28 7136 4413
info@ghpress.com
www.ghpress.com

A catalogue record for this title is available from the British Library.

Guildhall Press gratefully acknowledges the financial support of the Arts Council of Northern Ireland as a principal funder under its Annual Funding Programme.

ACKNOWLEDGEMENTS

My sincere thanks to everyone who helped me in so many ways to produce my debut novel and accompanying video. To Guildhall Press – Kevin Hippsley, Joe McAllister, Declan Carlin, Jenni Doherty, Peter McCartney, Jim Hughes and Paul Hippsley – for their expert guidance and professional input.

To my brother Michael Doherty and Gerard Brennan (crimesceneni.blogspot.com), Una McNally, Richard Moore, Pearse Moore, Peter Rozovsky (detectivesbeyondborders. blogspot.com), Aidan Lucid, Bill Vail and Don Mullan for their advice and support. To Vincent O'Callaghan for his compelling artistic video production. To all those in the legal profession for the endless sources of material I have drawn on to tell this story.

Very special thanks to Garbhan Downey for his continued encouragement and insightful editorial contribution. My appreciation is also due to the Arts Council of Northern Ireland for providing the opportunity for me to take this first step into writing. It was challenging but exciting. I hope I have done you all justice. Thank you.

For Clare

'Not for the whole treasure of your fathers,
all you enjoy, lands, flocks, or any gold
put up by others, would I hold my hand.
There will be killing till the score is paid.'
Homer, *The Odyssey*

CHAPTER 1

It was a beautiful May morning. Friday the thirteenth. William Bolton Black was hanging by the neck from the lower deck of Derry's steel-framed Craigavon Bridge. The tide, swollen the night before from a full moon, had raised the River Foyle and had almost touched Black's feet earlier that day.

The media arrived before the police, but because the death looked like a suicide they were in no rush to report it. They maintained a discreet and respectful distance. Derry, unfortunately, had had its unfair share of suicides recently, and the local journalists respected that. An unwritten agreement between them and the PSNI avoided unpleasant reportage. However, it would be difficult to keep this death low-key.

Detective Chief Inspector Jon Valberg surveyed the scene from the top of an old disused steam train that stood in the grounds of the nearby Foyle Valley Railway Museum. Tall in stature and dressed all in black – jeans, well-worn leather jacket and Rush T-shirt – Valberg cut an almost menacing figure. He deliberately made his thoughts known just to check who was listening to him.

'All he has on is that crimson sash thing. That's odd. Get plenty of photos. I'm glad someone had the sense to call a SOCO team. Do we know who he is yet? Anyone? Anyone know who he is, or will I just keep talking to myself?'

It was hard to block out the delicate process of removing Black's lifeless, naked body. His bulk made the task even more difficult. The recovery's slow pace gave the forensic team time to set up their white tarpaulin tent in the museum grounds. The sun rising over the city illuminated the tent and weak shadows were visible from inside.

Valberg watched, lost in thought, and his team knew to leave him alone. Just let him ramble on. Anyone who answered him did so at their peril. By now, uniformed PSNI officers had the area cordoned off. The upper and lower decks of Craigavon Bridge had been closed on Valberg's orders.

'Careful with the rope or whatever that is. I want to have a look at it,' Valberg shouted over to the scenes of crime officers as he climbed down from the train and made for the tent. He called Detective Constable Finbar Callaghan and Detective Sergeant Linda Wilson to join him. On his way, Valberg overheard a young uniform constable muttering to a colleague, 'What's up with him? Does he think the SOCO guys would throw the rope away?' Valberg stopped and asked him his name.

'Bell, sir. And, sir, I know the dead man,' the constable replied nervously.

Valberg told him to come with him.

As soon as the forensic team laid out Black's large frame in the tent Valberg recognised him. He'd thought it was him when he first saw the body hanging from the bridge and he'd let DS Wilson know. She was the most reliable member of his team.

Valberg gazed at the corpse in silence and ignored his fellow officer. His impatient and demanding reputation followed him. Many respected him, but many despised him; Valberg knew this and did not care. He was almost reckless in that regard, and this was often mistaken for arrogance. Valberg had a well-known history of alcohol abuse, suspensions and rows with every police officer in authority. He was a maverick in his work and in his personality. He was intense almost every second he was awake. When he slept, which was fitful and shallow, he only dreamt of dark and desperate things.

He was off his alcohol roller coaster at present but never forgot the dangers of a slip back into a world of depravity and personal mayhem. It was always close. Just ticking like a bomb in his head, ready to detonate at any time. A visit to Amsterdam or Marbella was always easy, and the hedonism that he enjoyed there always attractive. A quick flight out of Belfast International, a cab ride, then all the women and alcohol he wanted – almost enough to clear his head.

Eventually Valberg looked up at the others.

'Well, Constable Bell, what can you tell me about our body?'

Constable Bell was shaking. Valberg would not even look at him at first. The constable's voice was broken and nervous.

'The deceased is William Black, sir. He's an undertaker. Has a funeral parlour in the Waterside. Aged about sixty-five or so. He's an Apprentice Boy but not a bad fella really. No marching on the Walls this year for Billy, or the Sultan as he's known, sir. The Sultan of Bling. It seems he had a fondness for jewellery and money. He was always splashing it about. Don't think he would have had financial problems, but this recession is killing everyone, even people in the death business.'

Valberg looked at him and said, 'Thanks for that, Constable Bell. You're well ahead of me, then. But if I want your views on the deceased or the financial meltdown the world is in ...' he paused, 'or for that matter your opinion on the retention of evidence, I will ask for it. But that is helpful. At least someone here seems to know something. Now please step outside for a moment.'

Bell hurried out of the tent. Everyone else just looked intently at Black's body, anxious at this time to avoid eye contact with Valberg.

Valberg looked on as the sash around the Sultan was removed. The forensic team thought Valberg and his colleagues a nuisance as their cameras popped; their sighs made their irritation obvious. Valberg did not really care what they thought. After all, he was in charge.

Valberg looked at DC Callaghan and DS Wilson.

'He's as white as a ghost,' Valberg said. 'Look at the incision to the right of his neck. Look at the cuts to the palms of his hands, under his armpits, and look at the back of his heels. You would think a deranged physician attacked him. I bet his neck isn't even broken. We'll know later. I'm afraid the Sultan was tortured – and then killed – somewhere else. This will be a nightmare with the media and our friends in the political world. A complete nightmare.'

Everyone was stunned. No-one had thought anything but

suicide by an overweight man tormented by something. Something so horrific it caused him to kill himself by hanging.

A young female forensics officer in a white-hooded suit stepped forward to examine the body more closely. DS Wilson introduced her.

'This is Abigail Burns, sir, she's a friend of mine. We were at Foyle and Londonderry College together.'

Abigail turned momentarily, nodded at Valberg then returned to the corpse. A few seconds later she faced Valberg and spoke.

'Most of his blood is gone.'

Abigail took a deep breath to compose herself and continued her assessment.

'Those cuts are so precise. He may have been alive when it was all being done. He could have survived for twenty to thirty minutes. There's no blood on the ligature or the bridge. And I don't think his neck's broken, either. Detective Valberg, you will have it all as quick as I can manage, but you're right. It's murder. Not suicide. Hanging didn't kill him. There isn't enough bruising. The heart needs to be pumping. I suspect he was dead long before he ended up hanging under Craigavon Bridge. And just one more thing.'

'Yes. What is it?' asked Valberg.

'His ankles. Look. Ligature marks here, too. I think he was hung up. Both ankles together, judging by the marks there.'

Valberg continued to stare at the body.

DC Callaghan and DS Wilson knew well enough by now to let their boss do as he always did. Valberg needed time to think before he spoke. It would all come in time, and the practical, immediate matters needed attending to. That would leave Valberg time to wrestle with his cluttered thoughts. It took ages for him to reorganise and rationalise a crime scene in his head.

'I'll stay here for a while,' Valberg said. He was in no mood to visit the Black family. 'Do you mind if—'

'No problem,' DS Wilson said. 'Finbar and I will visit the deceased's family.'

'Thanks, Linda. We can all meet later. Four, at the office, to give us all time. Send Constable Bell up to me.'

'*Up* to you?'

'Yes. Up on the bridge. Wait until I walk up and look around for a while. Make that clear to him.'

'I understand.'

'Thank you, Linda. And, Finbar, find out everything you can about the Sultan. Everything. Any convictions for anything or any complaints or allegations about anything ever. Financial or sexual. Anything at all. Obviously, any other clubs or organisations he was in. You know?'

'We know, Jon.' Linda said. 'We'll ask his family about any threats or trouble as well and find out as much as we can in the meantime.'

'Could it be someone from his past? Someone not happy about the Sultan's services? Or maybe even a fellow Apprentice Boy? It had to be someone with pure and utter evil in mind to cut up a defenceless human being like this,' Valberg muttered. He was self-absorbing already.

Valberg allowed his mind to drift as he exited the tent and walked to the bridge. Drifting and playing devil's advocate frequently made people around Valberg feel awkward. He knew he was intense most of the time and he frightened people when he lost his temper. Maybe he was dangerous when in this state, too. As he got older, he was learning to control his temper more, concerned that if he lost it with the wrong person he might get a hammering. So he grew even more intense and insular and self-sufficient. It was all he could do. He had reached as far as he was going in the police now and as far as he wanted to go. He felt detached, but he really needed the PSNI and everyone around him. Inside, he knew he needed that support.

DS Wilson spoke with Constable Bell and found out where the Sultan lived. As she made to leave with DC Callaghan, Bell asked, 'What's he doing, Sarge?'

'Digging. He's digging.'

Constable Bell looked confused. He shook his head and raised his eyebrows. Constable Bell lacked Valberg's education or experience but he was wise enough to know when not to say too much or anything at all. It was a valuable trait. He was learning that it was always best in the police to keep your mouth shut, your head down and do your work.

'Whatever,' Bell said.

CHAPTER 2

Valberg stood with his hands behind his back at the entry to the lower deck of Craigavon Bridge, looking towards the Waterside. All was quiet now. Traffic was blocked in both directions. Valberg had it all to himself as the police photographers and forensic people had moved on to check the surrounding area.

This was his murder honeymoon, the period before the media got hold of the situation. Not the truth but a story. By now, or soon enough, Valberg knew someone innocently or otherwise from the PSNI would have leaked the identity of the deceased and that he had been murdered. No point in fretting over it. Just enjoy the brief honeymoon. He was adept and experienced enough to know the PSNI leaked like a sinking ship and always would.

Valberg was examining the framework of the bridge in the weak sunlight and imagining its construction. He studied it meticulously, realising he had driven across one of the few double-decker bridges in Europe so many times but never really appreciated how strong and sturdy it was.

In the near silence, Valberg's thoughts drifted and he murmured to himself the words of one of Seamus Heaney's more personal poems *Scaffolding*: 'Never fear/We may let the scaffolds fall/Confident that we have built our wall'. He thought these fine words reflected his confidence in the bridge's construction.

Heaney's poetry had always been a source of comfort and inspiration to Valberg. Just like his father, he could always mentally recite his work with the poet's rich voice in his head. He recalled the day he got into trouble with Father Doherty at school for having the temerity to suggest that poetry should not be interpreted so literally. Valberg thought the reader should discover their own meaning from it, not simply accept what any teacher dictated. When his father found out about this challenge to academic authority he insisted Jon apologise to Father Doherty immediately.

As Valberg looked down at the river, he thought of the violence, terror and fear of Billy Black's last moments. If Lucifer existed, this must surely be his work.

Valberg was unsure whether the murder was pure sectarianism. He didn't know whether this was good or bad from an investigative point of view. But if not sectarianism, what could it be? The murder was bewildering. Why would anyone want to go to all this trouble? If Billy Black had been tortured elsewhere, why not just leave him there? Valberg believed in logic but had difficulty understanding the rationale for this hateful murder.

Just then, Valberg noticed a large black rat scurry across a sewer pipe down to his right. He shivered, an involuntary action. As the tide eased now, fragments of what had once seemed important surfaced, decayed, ravaged by time and tides. A shopping trolley and a child's bike were stuck in the mud and tar beside the pipe. What a disgusting embankment, Valberg thought. What a disgusting place to die, alongside rusted metal and sewer rats.

Valberg wondered how Black was brought to the scene and his body dumped. It was possible, but no more than possible, for one very strong and fit individual to manage to get the Sultan over the bridge. But throwing such a heavy-built man over the lower deck of Craigavon Bridge quickly enough to avoid detection would surely have required the help of two people, Valberg thought. Wouldn't it?

Constable Bell watched quietly from below and obeyed his instructions exactly – that is until he saw Valberg climb onto the outside of the bridge. He seemed to be examining the ironwork around where Black had been hanging. Suddenly he slipped and jerked back. Constable Bell watched Valberg just about save himself from falling. Raising his hands, he shouted, 'Sir! Sir! Jesus, be careful, sir!'

It really was as if no other police officer cared about Valberg. They watched and shook their heads. Constable Bell made his way up to join Valberg.

Still looking down, Valberg cursed, '*Blodigt helvete*. It was the rat that made me slip. It was down there looking up at me. I had an awful nightmare recently, Constable. A real bad one. One of my worst in recent times. I was in the mouth of a rat. I was trapped and couldn't get out. This big bloody rat. The rat's litter was in there, too. I had to eat the litter to survive and then eat through the rat to get out. Bloody awful. Poor Billy Black. All he had was that damned rat to keep him company. The last time I was here, Constable, I thought I was saving a young girl from drowning. I was off duty and noticed her down there in the tar and mud, sort of rolling around. I thought it was strange and went down. Before I was about to climb down, she called me everything. Things I won't repeat, and she didn't even know I was a policeman.'

'Yes, sir. I get a lot of that here. Was she okay?'

'Okay? She said she was trying to get admitted to Gransha Hospital and was doing a pretend-suicide thing and I was messing it up. She said she had to put on her Victoria Beckham jeans to do it so the doctor would believe she was serious. Anyway, I left and phoned the police myself thinking she *should* be admitted to Gransha. But no matter. Poor girl. I had to get offside. I think she may have detected something of the fermented liquor on my breath. I would have been arrested myself. Again. Ah, well. Poor girl. Wonder how she is now. Good looking as well, in fact … Naw, fuck that now. I never saw her again. Never. Strange in a town like Derry.'

Constable Bell kept his mouth shut. He had never encountered a policeman, or anyone else for that matter, like Valberg before.

Valberg had just done what only those close to him encountered occasionally, especially in a tense investigation. After a moment of rudeness, Valberg would confess something personal. It would not be anything deeply personal. It was just like a small gift. A token of his thought process to compensate for his rudeness. It was his way of apologising.

'Okay,' Valberg said, and he climbed back over the railing

14

onto the roadway of the bridge. He looked at Constable Bell and asked him his first name.

'Michael, sir.'

'That's an important name for a policeman. A heavy one, too.'

'Why, sir?'

'Don't you know? Michael, our patron saint. Ever heard of the Policeman's Prayer?'

'No, sir. Sorry. I'm not very religious.'

'Neither am I, Michael, but the prayer says the policeman's lot is not a happy one.'

Valberg shook his head.

'In a way, I suppose, neither was Mr Black's. It's possible, just possible, as long as the body is prepared elsewhere, that one man could get it over the edge. You would need to be strong, but with the blood drained out of Billy, perhaps he would not have been so heavy. Maybe not. We'll find out later. Perhaps. One stop in the right vehicle, the rope already attached. One pull out and he is over, down with the rat, mud and stuff. But not so quick. You would have to get the body out and over. Not just down. Someone strong and fit might be able to do it. Just one big almighty heave. What do you think, Michael?'

'It's possible I suppose, sir.'

'Anything's possible. Let's walk east,' Valberg said.

Valberg talked and Constable Bell listened. As soon as they got to the lower deck, east side, a female constable on traffic control whom Bell recognised as Jennifer Hastings greeted both men. She knew Bell personally.

'Hello, Michael!' she called.

He put up his hand to acknowledge her. Valberg turned and walked back westwards. Constable Bell followed, listening to Valberg grow animated about shopping trolleys, rats, rubbish, mud, the suicide rate in Derry, Lord Craigavon and the concert he'd attended the day before in Dublin. When they got back to where the Sultan had been found, Valberg asked Bell to go and see what he could find out from the staff at the railway museum and let him know at his office later.

'No problem, sir, I'll be there.'

Bell headed back to what had become the white base

camp. He was trying to sort out everything that Valberg had talked about. He would have to write it all up in his notebook later which really worried him.

Valberg was to a degree a shy man. He knew the second he stepped off the bridge the press would be hounding him for answers and the politicians would be offering the most provocative condemnations they could come up with shortly after the true picture was unofficially revealed to them. He could see the gathering masses and wished he could just slip away unseen. But it was not to be. He had to do that thing all professionals hate. He had to be professional when he least wanted to.

Valberg was experienced enough to know that it is better to say nothing at all – not even 'no comment' – when endeavouring to leave a crime scene, especially when he was not sure what the crime was. So he decided not to engage with the media that had gathered. Don't contribute to the hysteria, thought Valberg. He should keep himself quiet, calm, dignified and, above all, professional. The truth will out eventually. It always does, for good or bad.

Valberg walked, unknowingly, into the start of what was to become a hurricane of murder, terror, bloodshed and unadulterated evil.

CHAPTER 3

Valberg's pristine black Saab 900 stood out from the other vehicles in the railway museum car park. Valberg was so proud of it, realising Saab were facing bankruptcy like the world in general and himself personally. He had the car fitted with a state-of-the-art sound system from Bang & Olufsen that was probably worth more than the vehicle itself. But he needed it for his music, and nothing but the best would do. Valberg's intention was to head for Strand Road Police Station as fast as the Saab could take him. Alderman Lionel Savage of the Democratic Unionist Party was in the media scrum with his back to Craigavon Bridge, doing what was probably the first of many interviews.

One journalist, Amanda Cleary from the *Derry Journal*, knew Valberg well and she watched him reject any calls for comment from the media in his forced polite way. The rest of the journalists just focused on what they could get. That was Alderman Savage.

Amanda had covered a story years earlier when Valberg was a detective constable in the Royal Ulster Constabulary and part of the team dealing with the Janice Sloan case. Amanda was aware that it had profoundly affected Valberg at the time.

* * *

Nineteen-year-old Janice Sloan had stumbled upon a row between two drunk men over a bottle of Mundies wine in her own drug-induced, inebriated state. In the altercation, one of the men got stabbed. A small kitchen knife was found later by Valberg at the scene on the opposite side of Craigavon Bridge from where the Sultan had been discovered, just above the embankment. Even though his blood was everywhere, the alcoholic survived. By the time the police arrived, the other alcoholic had gone and Janice Sloan was the only person who remained. She was arrested and later charged with attempted murder. She was high on Ecstasy and vodka herself and had no idea what was happening.

Valberg sat in on the police interview led by DS Victor Campbell Montgomery. Janice categorically denied the allegation of attempted murder as much as she could understand it. Valberg could only stare at the horrific results of the self-harm and mutilation on Janice's arms. The female solicitor sitting in on the interview shook her head as she watched him count the number of different cuts. Janice spent most of the time looking at Valberg's long hair – unusual for a policeman at that time – and his rumpled Rush T-shirt.

Montgomery represented everything old and used about the Royal Ulster Constabulary. Montgomery hated Janice. He did not want to be in the interview room with her. He hated solicitors as well. He despised them and treated them with contempt and disrespect. No matter how experienced the solicitors were, he would always say to them, just before the interview was about to begin: 'I don't see much of you in here doing this sort of thing. Are you new?'

Then he would start the formality of the interview. His poisonous comment was designed to undermine the solicitors in front of their clients. Most with sense just ignored him.

Montgomery was wrapping up the interview with Janice Sloan when he asked Valberg if he had any questions, assuming he would not. Valberg made an error both with his boss and with the female solicitor. He paused as the solicitor and Montgomery glared at him then asked, 'Janice. Are you okay? Is everything alright? What happened to your arms?'

Montgomery shifted uncomfortably in his seat, but the female solicitor was quick to respond.

'My client's wellbeing is neither here nor there with respect to the RUC. Please confine yourself to the matter at hand. Have you a question or not about the alleged offence?'

Janice was trying to answer. Apart from her solicitor, Valberg was the only person who had asked her if she was alright. The police doctor had treated her as a contemptible nuisance.

'Look. She's trying to answer. Let her answer,' Valberg pleaded.

A row broke out while Janice fixed her stare on Valberg. Janice waited until the puerile legal argument calmed.

'I'm okay, Mr Valberg. Thanks for asking. Sound man.'

But she was not 'okay', as Montgomery declared he was charging her with attempted murder.

'But we have nothing, sir. Nothing,' insisted Valberg.

Montgomery asked the solicitor to take Janice to the consultation room for a short break, as he wished to speak to his 'fellow officer'. As soon as they left he turned on Valberg.

'You listen here, Mr Fucking-ABBA-Fernando-Dancing Queen. Val-fucking-Mal or whatever they call you, you interloper. What the fuck are you anyway? American, Swedish or Irish? Nah, you're a Brit like me and the rest of us and your ma's a Taig. Your great Swedish da and Taig ma from Londonderry bring you to this shite hole with all the scumbags in it. Who'd fuckin' believe anyone born in the good old USA would want to come here? Then you get a law degree and join the police, you fuckin' long-haired lover from Liverpool. Are you for real? You're the Londonderry Yank now, alright. You have your ma to thank for that. Eh, boy? You fuckin' ask a question like that again with your fuckin' Yank accent or whatever it is, and I'll kick your fuckin' arse from here to America. We have a knife. Remember? You found it. It was you. It's bagged and tagged and off to forensics on the slow train for a minimum six months. She is charged and in custody. We will object to bail on the grounds of waiting for forensics on the knife. That is you, fuckwit. Your knife that you found. Her disgusting fingerprints might be on it or they might not. Frankly, my dear chum, I don't give a fuck, and she can rot in Maghaberry. In the meantime, she's off the streets while we deal with terrorists. You have a problem with that or me, Mr Supertrooper? Val. Fuck, what a stupid name. Just like you. Stupid.'

Then it got even worse.

'I don't care what you think of me,' said Valberg. 'I suppose you claim you're Irish when you're in America, eh? Your Irish passport tucked next to your Brit one in your pocket.'

'Fuck you, Val.'

'That girl needs help. She needs a hospital. If anything bad happens to her in Maghaberry I will say as much in the witness box in the Coroner's Court.'

'Get the hell out of my interview room, you fuckwit.'

Valberg stood in the corridor of the custody suite of Strand Road Station, listening to the uncontrollable crying from Interview Room 1 as Montgomery charged Janice with the scheduled offence of attempted murder. Valberg and the female solicitor could do nothing. No bail would be allowed in the Magistrates' Court, and there was no chance of even a sympathetic judge in the High Court releasing her on bail while a forensic report on the part of the prosecution was outstanding.

Bail was applied for, opposed and rejected.

Janice hanged herself on her first night in prison.

Rumour within the police was that Valberg had suffered some sort of mental breakdown as a result and hit rock bottom when it was revealed six months later that Janice's fingerprints were not even on the knife he had found. It badly affected him: his appetite for alcohol increased. It got rapidly worse after the inquest when he told the coroner everything that had happened and been said in the police station.

'I'll get that fucker Valberg,' Montgomery had spat. 'Wait and see. I'll get that fucker.'

* * *

Amanda Cleary picked her moment carefully. Just as the media focused on Savage, she called Valberg softly as he was about to get into his car.

'Jon. Jon, remember me?'

Valberg looked around.

'Amanda. Yes, of course I do. You're still with the *Irish News* then?'

'No, I've been with the *Derry Journal* for a while now.'

'That's good. I remember you did great work on Janice

Sloan's case. You covered the inquest well, too.'

'A long time ago, Jon. It's different now.'

'Is it really?' asked Valberg. 'I dunno. Sometimes I think ... well, that's not for now. I better go. Take care, Amanda.'

Amanda Cleary was quietly content that she had renewed a valuable contact in a story she sensed would be big. She had nothing for her editor yet but she was confident that would soon change. She watched Valberg closely – and he knew it. He also knew not to stand talking to her in front of all the other journalists. She would wait. The macabre murder of an Apprentice Boy was enough for the hysteria to begin.

'Bye, Jon. You take care, too.'

Valberg's Saab 900 roared away.

The music inside it roared, too. *The Grudge* by Tool.

CHAPTER 4

Valberg took over the operations room at Strand Road Station as a secure base for his team to deal with the Billy Black case. By now, lurid accounts of a sectarian murder in Derry were rampant in the media. Valberg did everything he could to avoid the news on television and radio. Even when he was in his car he only listened to music.

Information was coming thick and fast from other police and detectives.

DC Callaghan confirmed that Black had no previous convictions and not one allegation or complaint, sexual or otherwise, existed.

'He seems to be nothing more than a hard-working man. Nothing on him at all. An Apprentice Boy, yes. But that's not a crime. They've around a hundred thousand members, I understand. They all have to join up in the Memorial Hall on Society Street.'

DS Wilson outlined what was known of Black's last movements.

'His wife, Sylvia, says he got up very early at around four o'clock to go to his parlour at Black's Funeral Home on Limavady Road to do some work. It was a regular thing if he had a funeral that day. A Walter Watson was due to be buried and his body was kept there overnight. We believe that's where Black was killed. Forensics are still there now. They should be finished soon.'

'Okay, I'll go later, then.'

'I'll get you the new access code, it's one of those keypad entry systems. Jon, forensics say there are signs the door mechanism was tampered with but there are no traces of blood there. Not a drop. The only thing was a hook left in the ceiling. Well placed and secure. I noticed it right away. They are working on it. So it was just Walter Watson and, well ... well, I thought it was odd. Twelve empty coffins, arranged in a circle. It looked strange. The killer must have done it. Then Mr Watson. So thirteen. It looks like Mr Black was hung from the ceiling in the centre of the coffins and sliced open bit by bit. All his blood must have flowed out of him there until he died. Awful. A sheet or something had to be placed on the ground and removed. It just had to be. A sheet or tarpaulin. Something had to be used to collect the blood and then disposed of.'

'But why, Linda? What a hassle.'

Linda shook her head.

'I don't know. This is as bizarre as it gets. But the killer, or killers, must have been waiting for him. That's where the evidence, such as it is, takes us now.'

'And we go where the evidence goes, do we?'

'There is no other logical explanation, Jon. As far as I can see anyway.'

Valberg shuddered inside and turned to Constable Bell. 'Anything useful from the museum?'

'Nothing really, sir.'

Constable Bell was nervous reading from his notebook.

'No CCTV, either, sir. I checked. I know the boys who do all that CCTV stuff. There was some problem with the entire system all over Derry last night. They said it's not the first time recently. I'm checking all that and our own CCTV footage as well. But nothing yet. I'll keep at it. It had to be under cover of darkness, sir. Had to be. Or just before dawn. Oh, and a wino – sorry, sir – an alcoholic gentleman who approached me at the museum was quite insistent I tell you something.'

Everyone looked away as Constable Bell read from his notebook with only Valberg looking at him.

'Well, sir, he said you knew him and – I am just reading from my notes, sir – he said, "You fucking tell Valberg I stabbed Fonsi McCloskey on the embankment and that Montgomery guy didn't want to know." Sorry, sir, but he is of no fixed abode. He was quite insistent I tell you. And, sir, the thirteen DS Wilson mentioned. Well, probably nothing, but wasn't it—'

'Thirteen on the day, Bloody Sunday,' DC Callaghan interjected, 'but one died later from his wounds.'

'Well, no,' said Constable Bell. 'I mean, aye, that's right, but I was referring to the siege of Derry. Wasn't it thirteen men then that closed the gates?'

'Apprentice Boys, but, yes. Michael is right,' Callaghan confirmed.

Valberg watched the exchange closely.

'Nothing worse than a motiveless murder. Sectarianism is the easy solution to that.'

That was as much as they got out of Valberg.

It was getting close to six in the evening. He told Constable Bell and DS Wilson to make their way to the Apprentice Boys Memorial Hall and find out more about Billy Black.

'Just dig. The usual, Linda. Me and Finbar will go to that funeral home shortly. I was going to go on my own, but, Finbar, you come. Bed and rest for all after. I might go back to the bridge. Keep in touch on the mobiles and I will see you all here in the morning. Okay?'

* * *

As she drove to the Memorial Hall DS Wilson listened to the six o'clock news on Radio Ulster. It prompted her to offer some advice to Constable Bell.

'Michael. Don't ever talk about what the radio or TV says about any case we are involved in to DCI Valberg. And definitely never mention what any politician says.'

Linda parked the car and turned the ignition off. Before Michael could respond, the sickening noise of a loud explosion shattered the air. Glass and debris from the Memorial Hall rained down on the car. Linda immediately feared for anyone caught in such a blast. They would not stand a chance.

Valberg called her instantly; he'd heard the explosion from the police car park as he'd been delayed leaving.

'Linda, what the fuck was that? Where are you? Are you okay?'

'We're okay, Jon. We're right outside the Memorial Hall. It sounded like a car bomb. I think it went off over in London Street.'

'I've got Finbar with me. We'll meet you there. We're on our way!'

CHAPTER 5

When Valberg and Finbar arrived in London Street the smouldering wreckage of what once had been a small family car lay enmeshed with the mangled wrought-iron gates of the historic St Columb's Cathedral. Valberg was initially relieved to see no obvious human remains in the wreckage or at the scene. Often a dismembered body, or something that resembled it, would be present and horrifically burnt beyond recognition. But nothing. He asked Finbar to supervise a search of the area, just in case some hapless victim had been flung onto a roof or into a back yard.

DS Wilson said that when she and Michael got to the scene they noticed the blast had been white-hot, not red. She told Valberg there was a haze of white from the car and that everything had just melted. The crater in the road was testament to the blast's force. The Fire Service people and the police forensic teams would work together to determine the type of explosives and the nature of the fire.

As Valberg and DS Wilson surveyed the area for evidence, an elderly white-haired man approached them. He was the caretaker for the Church of Ireland cathedral and was shaking. He held back tears as he told them in faltering words that his friend Avril Gibson had been in the car when it exploded. He had been chatting to her for a while in the cathedral grounds before she left and got into her car which had been parked close to the cathedral gates, less than two hundred yards from where DS Wilson had parked on Society Street. He went on to tell them about Avril, a retired

26

schoolteacher and a grandmother, and about her voluntary work for the cathedral.

Valberg and DS Wilson realised that Avril had had no chance. She had vanished like a vapour trail. At the age of sixty-nine, the mother of four children and seven grandchildren did not deserve to die as she did. She did not deserve such cruel obliteration, they thought.

Miraculously, no-one else was injured. It seemed planned that way. The words 'military precision' suggested themselves to Valberg. Buildings around Society Street, London Street and Pump Street suffered some damage, but the car had taken the brunt of the explosion.

Valberg was relieved Constable Bell and DS Wilson were unhurt, but as he stared at the mess, he knew a tidal wave of sectarian tension would now wash over the city; politicians would make certain of that.

Alderman Savage was first at the scene, saying that the Protestant community was once again under siege and that he suspected dissident republicans were involved. He had no evidence of this. The only things that linked the two murders were age and religion. Valberg had nothing else to go on. The Strand Road operations room now had another name added for investigation.

Valberg would never let his guard down. But he was truly horrified. He left his three subordinates to do what they could at London Street; he wanted to get away from the media. He drove straight to Black's Funeral Parlour on the Limavady Road.

The police were everywhere now with checkpoints at major junctions delaying traffic. A sense of unease and fear pervaded the air.

By the time he arrived at the funeral parlour the forensics and uniformed police had left, but the property remained sealed with police tape. Valberg's mobile rang as he parked. Linda had learned from Abigail Burns that Walter Watson's family had not been able to bury him as arranged that day so the body was still in the funeral parlour. She warned him that, for some reason, the coffin lid was open. She also confirmed the new alarm code at the building so he could gain access.

'How is it there with you?' asked Valberg.

'The usual. Savage being as critical of everyone as possible and helping none of us. The media are here, and there is talk of the Serious Crime Unit coming down from Belfast to oversee things. Just great. But people are scared, Jon. There is real tension here, I think, with two Protestants murdered. I hope there's no more.'

Valberg removed the police tape, tapped the code into the alarm pad and let himself in. Total silence filled the dimly lit funeral parlour.

The smell of death greeted Valberg. The Sultan had to have been tortured and murdered here, he thought. Valberg imagined him taped and forced to the ground and mutilated, squealing like a pig and bleeding like a pig and slaughtered like a pig. Then Valberg realised from the police tape on the ceiling and from what Linda had said earlier that he must have been tied up by the ankles as the blood left his body. The more he fought, the more he squealed for mercy, the faster and harder his heart would have pumped and the blood gushed. The Sultan would have seen and felt his life flowing out of him. With no traces of blood anywhere to be found, the killer was professional and meticulous.

Valberg sat on a chair and noticed the things that make up a working life and the tools of Billy's trade. Amid all the death around him, pictures of Billy's grandchildren cluttered his desk. A yellow Post-it note was stuck beside the phone. It read: 'Watson for Embal. DNF!'

Valberg could not resist going to look at Walter Watson's freshly embalmed corpse. He could smell the various fluids used in the process emanating from the flesh.

Valberg spoke softly. 'My only witness, Walter. Well, what can you tell me? What did you see, Walter? Can you give me a description? Anything at all?'

He stared at the corpse. Walter Watson was dead for sure. Just a lump of lifeless flesh, cold and gaunt. Valberg thought about rats again. He was fighting sleep, as all he'd dreamt about recently was a rat's mouth.

The funeral parlour was so quiet and peaceful. Valberg did the unthinkable. He lay down on the floor of the room where Billy had been tortured, surrounded by twelve empty coffins, his only company Walter Watson, deceased. Thoughts of the recent murders ran through his mind, but he was peaceful and content. He went through the events that might have left Billy Black's body hanging on Craigavon Bridge. It would have taken an extremely fit and able individual to carry out everything on his own. But a lone killer was all Valberg could imagine now. His gut instinct was nagging him. Valberg saw his reflection in the polished silver coffin handles. The last thing he thought he would be doing today was lying exhausted on an undertaker's floor surrounded by coffins and a dead body.

Valberg imagined the Sultan swinging above him and a sharp knife blade picking its moment to cut with precision. The seduction of the silence around him dulled his senses and his mind drifted. Suddenly a scraping noise close by jerked him back to his feet. He drew his pistol and scanned the parlour.

'Who's there?'

Nothing. He checked everywhere. It must have been a cat – or a rodent, he thought.

Valberg had been in there a long time, longer than he'd thought. It was going on four in the morning. It was time to go; back out and away from the serenity and company of Walter Watson and the peace he instilled. He locked up and carefully replaced all the police cordon tape on the outside of the door.

At full volume, Valberg listened to Led Zeppelin's *No Quarter* on his way back to London Street as dawn began to break.

CHAPTER 6

The forensic team at London Street were still working under spot lamps and had Gibson's wrecked car cocooned in a white tent. Valberg hoped that it would be preserved properly and not left lying to rust. Proper and legal preservation of evidence was sacrosanct to him. He had concerns – for rational or irrational reasons – that there would be a problem with the legal, evidential weight of what was left of the car. This would usually happen the day before a trial was to start. The chief investigating officer would incur the judge's wrath and the defence barrister's sarcastic comments. It would be ignominious and unacceptable for Valberg but he had experience of some of his colleagues lying in court and not caring at all about a case collapsing.

Valberg had been at the scene for a few hours when he got an anxious call from DC Callaghan who was up in Creggan. Paddy Sharkey, aged sixty-six, was missing from his home at Rinmore Drive. His bedroom looked like an abattoir. Blood everywhere. It was a terrible sight. Callaghan's voice was trembling.

'I'm on my way,' Valberg barked. 'Just don't let anyone near the bedroom, or the house for that matter, Finbar.'

Fatigue and tension gripped Valberg. He sensed instinctively that this must be somehow linked to the other two murders. This kind of thing hadn't happened in Derry since the worst of the Troubles. He wondered briefly whether it was wise to drive to Rinmore on his own, especially in a car as recognisable as his. But Valberg had taken chances before, too many to count, and this was an emergency.

He sped past Long Tower Church and through the Bog-side which slept like a concrete lion waiting to be set free. Daylight spread across the huddled terraced houses as he raced up the hill to Creggan.

Valberg drove up Iniscarn Road and turned right into Linsfort Drive leading up to the top of Rinmore Drive. He knew the area well.

A crowd had gathered outside Paddy Sharkey's home, including some well-known, and malcontent, republicans as the PSNI generally viewed them. Valberg gathered himself before he got out. Thankfully, Finbar was there to meet him. Yet another platoon of forensic people were already at work.

A local councillor called Dermot Kyle confronted Valberg.

'No stone left unturned here, Mr Valberg, eh? What are you gonnie do now?'

'Hello, Dermot.'

Valberg knew acknowledging the councillor on first-name terms would keep him quiet and undermine him in the presence of many supporters of the dissident republicans.

Valberg walked into the narrow, newly renovated Northern Ireland Housing Executive property. The place was full of police.

'Where is it, Finbar?'

'Straight up left, sir. Right up those stairs to the back bedroom.'

'Finbar, get a screen organised to the front of the house. No more bloody rubber neckers or gossip merchants. Do it now.'

Valberg immediately regretted his choice of words. Blood, blood and more blood. Soaked into everything. Splattered over everything. The smell was stomach wrenching. Two policemen looked in, turned around and vomited, much to the forensic team's annoyance. Valberg knew the photographs would be even worse than the reality. The rooms were small and the landing tight. It was hard to stay out of the way. Valberg looked out the back window.

'Jesus, that's a lovely garden. He has all sorts growing there. Potatoes and onions, carrots and other stuff. Good man, Paddy. What a shame,' said Valberg. He stood silent for a few seconds, gazing, thinking, then snapped back to the moment.

Valberg turned to DC Callaghan. 'He let the blood flow everywhere this time. Deliberately. This room is a mess. How did the neighbours not hear anything? Or did they? Get all that organised, Finbar. Get uniform to do it. You go back to the office. I don't want you here too long. Right? We'll go now and let forensics get on with it.'

'Sir, I know it's a stupid question, but is this a missing-person case or a murder?'

'Subject to your religious views, Finbar, the divine living human being that once was Paddy Sharkey is no more. It looks like a murder to me. We just need to find the corpse to prove it.'

Valberg made his way downstairs and into the front living room. He lifted what appeared to be a note neatly placed behind a ticking Smiths clock on the mantelpiece of the living room. Valberg read: 'Two baps, the *Irish News*, two pints of milk, bread and half-pound mince and a packet of custard creams if change.'

All meticulously written in first-class handwriting.

Uniformed police watched.

Valberg then went over to a glass china cabinet full of ornaments and family pictures and found Paddy's phone and electricity bills with a note on top: 'Pay Monday.'

Valberg paused. No-one dared interrupt him as he stood in Paddy Sharkey's front living room, examining everything about Paddy's world. Valberg thought about the stupid things in life that we worry about. Now in death all meaningless.

A copy of the 1916 Easter Proclamation of the Irish Republic hung above the fireplace. Under it, on a little wooden shelf, was a piece of stone with 1973 marked on the front. It looked like masonry stone. Valberg lifted it and whispered to no-one in particular: 'Nineteen seventy-three. The year the IRA blew up Walker's Pillar on the city Walls.'

Valberg examined the stone, realising he held a piece of history in his hands and remembering how an effigy of Colonel Lundy, the so-called siege traitor, used to be burnt from the pillar every year for decades until it came crashing down. He carefully replaced the memento as Paddy's distraught relatives arrived. The honeymoon was over.

Valberg had seen enough to get a sense of Paddy Sharkey's life. He began to think how ordered and structured it was, unlike his own chaotic existence. Neat rows of vegetables growing happily and an orderly system of bill paying and a note of what to buy, especially the 'custard creams, if any change'. This was the simple life of a non-offensive pensioner who could harm no-one. Valberg admired the pride Paddy so obviously took in his garden. He thought how important Paddy's last notes were to him and how meaningless they were now.

The mayhem outside was getting louder and the gathering crowd more agitated. Not without reason, thought Valberg. The crowd hated the police as much as they ever did. Nothing had changed. The venom against the PSNI was palpable. Everyone involved knew that time, as ever, was of the essence and that the quicker they got out of the area the better.

The media were gathering now, Valberg's signal to go. Fear was gripping Derry, a reminder of the fear thirty years of conflict had created.

As Valberg left, he saw Father James Doherty arriving, older now and grey, like a man who had had enough. Enough of everything, including religion and God. He still made a cutting figure all in black, but he was a long way from the man he had been. Valberg wondered whether illness drained him or whether he, like Valberg, was just tired, tired of everything. The priest noticed Valberg as he consoled the family but knew better than to stop him slipping away.

Father Doherty's arrival allowed Valberg an easy escape. Valberg was grateful. Not for the first time, religion saved him.

CHAPTER 7

On his way back to Strand Road Station, Valberg got a call from DS Wilson.

'I've just spoken to my friend Abigail, from the SOCO team. She's been at all the murder scenes so far. Nothing official yet, but she knows how long these things take and she is trying to help. They found Mr Sharkey's blood type mentioned on his medical papers. O positive. He had a note of all his medication. You know, stuff like Ramipril for blood pressure and that. I've just been told and—'

'Hold on, Linda, I have a call coming in from Finbar. Yes, Finbar. I'm on with Linda here. Can you be quick?'

Then Valberg realised he had driven into the Bogside so he pulled over and stopped.

'They've found him, sir. Or part of him.'

'What?'

'His head, sir. Paddy Sharkey's head. It's stuck up on the metal railings on what's left of Walker's Pillar. On the Walls. Facing the wee church, St Augustine's. I've just had a call from there.'

'I'll go straight up now.'

He got back to Linda and told her about Sharkey's head.

'Linda, I need you up there soon as possible. I have to go.'

'But, sir. Jon, I need to tell you what Abigail said. It's unofficial, but they can do these tests now at the scene. They have these devices with them now. Electronic stuff, handheld, that can check blood types. You probably didn't even notice Abigail up there. She just called me. The delay is all bluff. You know, waiting on results from Belfast and all that crap. The blood up there in Rinmore, Jon. It's not Paddy Sharkey's blood. It's not even human. Abigail says it's animal blood. What does it mean, Jon?'

'Jesus Christ. He's playing with us. This is no sectarian bloodbath. It's something else. This can't get any worse. Can it?'

Linda avoided the question and said she would see him on the Walls.

Something snapped inside Valberg. A strange sensation seemed to pass through him like a ghost. He had a real feeling of unease deep in his abdomen. He sat motionless in his car, gripping the steering wheel and grinding his teeth.

Valberg was sinking. He craved a drink. Any alcoholic substance. Just anything. He could taste it. That adolescent angst built up inside him. But he was older now. Always expect the unexpected. Trust no-one. Believe nothing. Rely on no-one. Expect no gratitude. Treat everyone with suspicion, including all family. Life is dark, black and unforgiving. Life is nasty, brutish and short. There is no such thing as law and order. There is no justice. There is no truth. There is no afterlife, either, for anyone. That is a bluff, too, and a fairy story. When you think human beings can get no more depraved, they do. Srebrenica happened. The Spanish Civil War happened. Murdered bodies buried all over Spain. There is no point in having any faith in humanity. There is no right to life. We are all vulnerable and liable to breakdown, and no-one cares about anyone. Each and every one of us is selfish and greedy. We can all kill and we are all angry most of the time. Happy people delude themselves but not others. Life is empty, and with death there are empty homes, empty spaces and empty corners. Everything is desolate and there is no hope.

Valberg could see in bold capitals on the front of his medical file RISK-BIPOLAR. He was aware he was at risk of having a bipolar disorder and accepted it.

Alcohol usually wiped such thoughts away. Just one drink. Valberg had made one step to recovery. He stopped carrying two flasks of vodka and orange juice with him everywhere he went. That was progress; safer for him and the public.

Valberg felt like a fool. These irrational and damaging

messages to his brain did not help his health. He was in such a dark place he thought music could not even save him. He thought it could not get worse, but it did.

As he sat parked on Westland Street looking up at the Walls and imagining Paddy Sharkey's decapitation, a woman in her late thirties came running and screaming down nearby Cable Street.

Valberg jumped out of his car and tried to calm her. Dominica McLaughlin pointed frantically to where she had come from and told Valberg she had just called to help her elderly mother but something terrible had happened in the house and she fled.

Valberg approached the house cautiously while a neighbour ushered Dominica away still sobbing. Valberg drew his pistol, very conscious of where he was in the heart of the Bogside.

Inside, he found Majella McLaughlin's wheelchair on its side on her living-room floor. Majella McLaughlin was hanging upside down, suspended by the ankles from the ceiling by what looked like a nylon rope. She was dead but her eyes were wide open, staring at the world. A set of rosary beads lay on the floor.

Valberg swore silently to himself, put his gun away and gently closed her eyes. He eased himself slowly onto the sofa facing the dangling corpse and called DS Linda Wilson.

'Change of plan, Linda. Come to Cable Street in the Bogside. We have another dead body.'

He could still hear Dominica screaming.

Two Catholics and two Protestants dead now. Each of them a defenceless pensioner. That was enough. No more. It could not get any worse.

CHAPTER 8

The first person on the scene in Cable Street was Father Doherty, who had been contacted by the neighbours. He stood next to Majella McLaughlin's body and began to pray in Latin, blessing her in what Valberg assumed was some form of the Last Rites of the Catholic Church.

Valberg did not care. He was weary and just glad to be sitting down for a while. His thoughts drifted to Carolina Munoz, a milky Latina beauty he visited often in Marbella. She professed to be religious and had shown Valberg photographs of her daughter's First Holy Communion. He felt no guilt about paying for her professional services but found the religious claims unsettling. He wondered if it was a scam to extract more money from clients. Valberg followed Carolina to the Catholic church she said she attended with her daughter Maria in San Pedro, southwest of Marbella town. He discovered she was a regular visitor and realised her faith was genuine. From then on Valberg insisted on having sex with Carolina only in hotel rooms; the religious pictures in the apartment she used to entertain clients disturbed him.

Father Doherty finished his prayers, blessed the body one last time and sat beside Valberg on Majella's couch. Valberg did not speak. With the dangers of sleep deprivation looming, he had found his most comfortable seat in days. But he felt out of place in this small room, in this small house in the Bogside. He found it difficult to even move. The house was full of religious artefacts, all seemingly staring at him.

Police and ambulances were arriving now, and the press and all the local politicians. Everything repeated itself. It was like murder Groundhog Day. Nothing had changed. Terror, evil, death and silence. Then discovery, panic, mayhem, police, forensics, press and politicians. Everything took the same course. Valberg had four horrific murders to deal with, carried out, it seemed, by the same person or persons.

There were no obvious cuts or marks on the body, apart from those left on her ankles by the rope. Trauma and fear had killed Majella McLaughlin. The killer may have thought about cutting her throat, but no. At least he spared her that. Majella was gaunt, grey and bony. She was no match for anyone. A strong man could have lifted her with one arm. Valberg could only wonder what sort of person would come into the home of a religious, enfeebled pensioner and inflict such suffering.

Father Doherty spoke to Valberg on his way out. 'What is going on, Jon? What hell has been opened? I heard some of the officers say they've found poor Paddy Sharkey's mutilated body up on the Walls. What human being could kill people in this way? What is the sense of it all? Why, Jon?'

'Father, I wish I had your faith but I sense doubt. It's not for me to say, but we have no time for debate now. You will have to leave. I can hear them all clamouring outside. I just wish – I really do – I wish I had your faith, Father. It might be easier then to deal with all this.'

Father Doherty was in no mood for prolonged discussion but his obvious anguish caused Valberg to wonder if the priest's faith was weakening. Valberg could see he was close to tears. Valberg respected him for this. But what was he really so emotional about? Valberg thought Father Doherty was like him, case hardened and devoid of emotion. Seemingly not.

Father Doherty steadied himself and said, 'Now is not the time, I know, but best wishes to your father. He's getting the best care he can get where he is. I might see you there. I know the process now and will get out of the way. We can speak later. Majella was a lovely woman and—'

'The work of the devil, Father? Has that Philistine god of Accaron you used to tell me about come to Derry for a while? Pure evil, if that makes sense.'

The two men in black stared at each other. Valberg was

well aware how much Father Doherty knew him and his family, especially his father. Valberg was old enough now to realise that the clash he had had with Father Doherty all those years ago was well forgotten.

'Perhaps later we can talk, Jon, but it's getting crowded now, and I know you're for the Walls. God bless you all.'

'Goodbye, Father. I'm glad you came, and perhaps you can help this lady's daughter as well. One of the neighbours is looking after her.'

Valberg remained seated, almost as if he had murdered Majella and was waiting for the police to come and arrest him. He heard Linda's voice at the front door enquiring where he was. He called out to her and she entered the room.

Linda took a sharp breath when she saw the corpse still suspended from the ceiling but her professionalism saved her.

'This is terrible. Another one. What's happening? How many more are we going to find?'

Valberg sighed and shook his head. He looked at Linda, fresh and showered, nothing like his own state.

'You need rest, Jon. Why don't you go home for a while?'

'Soon, Linda, soon. Any news?'

Linda said she had heard the Chief Constable was looking for Valberg and planning a trip to Derry.

'*Blodigt helvete*. And there was me thinking it couldn't get any worse,' quipped Valberg amid the hustle and bustle of another PSNI murder scene.

'Check the ceiling,' he finally said, 'and how the rope is secured. Another hook. Maybe we can lift something from them this time. I expect the cause of death to be a heart attack at best. Poor Majella and her family. No-one deserves this or what I am about to go and see. I want you, Finbar and Constable Bell up on the Walls. I want the four of us together up there. I'll find us a private place.'

'A what, Jon?'

'A private place that isn't bugged. The privileged and professional consultation rooms for the solicitors and their clients are bugged in the police station. Do you think they're not? I always keep my mouth shut in a police station. A good solicitor gave me that advice.'

CHAPTER 9

The rest of Paddy Sharkey's body was found on top of a grave slab in the grounds of St Augustine's Church opposite the Walker monument. Blood was everywhere, splattered about recklessly on the doors and walls of the ancient building. It had spilled over the concrete grave slab top as if the victim had been sliced open and offered up in a demonic pagan ritual. Sharkey's Catholic blood had soaked into the hallowed ground that had become his deathbed. He had surrendered himself in a churchyard so closely associated with the Protestant defenders of the city during the Great Siege laid centuries before by the Jacobites.

Derry was stunned by the nature of the four murders and outlandish rumours were doing the rounds. A senior citizens slayer was roaming the streets. A severed head had been found – with strange marks to the neck. A vampire was at large. That was Valberg's favourite. It was also a favourite of some of the media. 'Derry Vampire Murders' had a good non-sectarian ring to it as a headline.

But the most intriguing story began with a local astrologist claiming that the solar system's second largest planet, Saturn, had reached its near-thirty-year cycle around the sun and its unsettling influence was now overhanging Derry. She grimly forecast a time of judgement and death for the people of the city, a time when no-one would be safe. The Grim Reaper, she asserted, was merely facilitating the journey from death to the afterlife which, for many in Derry, would be to hell. Despite these warnings being mere fantasy, fear of the devil and evil itself gripped the city tightly.

The media tried, by police request, to be as careful as possible not to add to the hysteria. The *Derry Journal*'s website was already running with the question 'WHY?' as the banner headline in their news section above a detailed report on the murders and photographs of the deceased.

Amanda Cleary had compiled the piece as the story developed. She had written it as responsibly as she could. Now she was up on the Walls on a tip-off that she would be officially welcome if the Chief Constable visited.

By the time Valberg and the others arrived, a forensics tent already covered the area where Paddy lay though it had been difficult to put it up in the confined space near the entrance of the small church. Valberg entered and saw Abigail Burns who was down on her knees, examining the corpse.

'How the fuck did we miss all this? Jesus Christ. We've been all over this area. His body must have been here all that time. Do we know whose blood this is yet?' Valberg asked.

Abigail looked up at Valberg and spoke softly so no-one would hear. Uniformed police would pass on everything to their friends.

'Official or unofficial. Which do you want, Detective Valberg?'

Valberg hunkered down.

'The truth,' he said, knowing that if any other police heard him talking to Abigail that it would be embellished and leaked. 'The truth as you see it, if you can tell me. The truth in all its magnificent glory.'

Abigail paused and lowered her face mask slightly to enable her to speak.

'Officially, it's Mr Sharkey's blood ... and he is dead.'

'Officially. That's helpful.'

'Unofficially, with the amount of blood splatter around the headstones and grave slabs here and up to the church door, his heart was pumping when he was decapitated. Perhaps tortured alive, like Billy Black. I have to assume it was done here,' Abigail said.

'Right. I see that. Anything else?'

'Whoever did it would probably have used a butcher knife

and maybe a metal glove like butchers use to avoid injury to himself. And the deceased wasn't wearing any shoes, just his socks. He struggled so hard his heels tore through them and cut the back of his ankles on the slab.'

Valberg shook his head. 'Fuck me. *Blodigt* holy fucking *helvete.*'

'This was no messy internet-style decapitation. It was clean. Military style. A very sharp knife in a strong hand. Or two sets of strong hands at work. Two people maybe.'

'You really think so?'

'Maybe, but if pressed I would say one because if two people were involved, I would not expect to see the ankle injuries. He would have been held down tighter. Hard to say.'

'So, is it one or two?'

'I'm not sure.'

Valberg shook his head again.

'Decapitation isn't easy, especially when you get to the spinal column. Look at the clean cut. It's immaculate.'

'Looks like someone gutted a fish. Jesus. Sweet fucking hell.'

'The grave slab is unmarked apart from the heel marks, but halfway through the decapitation he must have lifted the victim up so the blade wouldn't leave a mark. Then the head came clean off. I can't find any blade or scratch marks on the slab. Nothing.'

'Where's the head?'

Abigail pointed to a plastic container at the side of the grave slab. 'Sorry. We had to get it down. I assure you we filmed it all for you. It was stuck on top of the railings right at the corner facing the church here. Well, in this direction anyway. Everything is preserved. I'm going to examine it more closely later.'

Valberg sighed as he got up.

'I waited patiently there without stopping your flow too much. I thought you were going to give me something even more unofficial.'

Abigail had opened a door now and could not close it. She stared at Valberg. 'It's not my exact area but I can tell you what I've heard.'

'Go on.'

'White phosphorus, only a bare ounce of Semtex and two bombs, one under Avril Gibson's seat and one at the petrol tank. Detonated at the same time. By remote control. No timer. The bomber was watching. She had no chance. Whoever killed these people had military training or even police training. And whoever tortured Billy Black knew what they were doing, too. I estimate he lost about eight pints of blood. Nearly a stone. It would have made him a little lighter, but perhaps not so noticeable for a strong individual, or two. My sense is that cutting Mr Black and letting him bleed to death was part of the torture. Probably nothing to do with making the body lighter.'

'A new celebrity diet.'

'What?'

'Losing blood. Get a fucking celebrity to say if you lose some of your blood, you will shed a few pounds and every fucking moron will be at it. Sorry. Just a thought ... Why white phosphorous? Surely he or they knew it would be found.'

'Cruelty. There was no need for it. Just like Black's torture. The Geneva Conventions outlaw its use against civilians.'

'The Americans used it in Fallujah in the Iraq War, didn't they?' Valberg asked.

'And the Israelis, in Gaza and Lebanon.'

'Complete cruelty, alright. Like the others. They could have been murdered easier,' said Valberg.

'Especially with their age, but this is real sadistic bloodletting. Putting a bomb in Gibson's car and blowing her up wasn't good enough,' said Abigail. 'I'm no profiler, but it doesn't take a genius to work out that you have a murdering, evil and vicious killer roaming Derry. Close to us all the time. The white phosphorous vaporised her. I've never heard of the use of it here. How could anyone get it? Perhaps an enemy within. I dunno. That's your job.'

'Someone with a military connection for sure is watching us. A recent military connection as well, it seems,' said Valberg.

'You find the link and I'll feed you what I can. Now you have the definite line-of-inquiry angle for the press. Follow it, I guess. Well, I hope that helps. I need more time here, then I'm going to look at Paddy's head.'

'Thanks, Abigail.'

Abigail stood and removed her mask and pulled her white hood back to reveal the face of a beautiful woman doing an ugly job. Together they exited the tent and went their separate ways.

CHAPTER 10

As Valberg left the grounds of St Augustine's Church he told Linda he wanted Abigail to meet with them all later at the nearby Double Bastion on the corner of the Walls.

'All together, Linda. Not separately. I'll wait there.'

Valberg walked south on Grand Parade to the Double Bastion, safe in the knowledge that uniformed police had the area cordoned off from the public. It was another beautiful, fresh day and Valberg found some rare space and time to think things over.

He watched Finbar and Linda at work and wondered if Finbar had got any sleep. He had told him more than once to go home, but he was still working. He knew Finbar was a huge GAA fan and must be missing all that was going on in that world.

Valberg only worked with people he liked. They were always different or unique and would attract criticism, like he did. He monitored Finbar's work closely, never telling him how much he admired him. Finbar never knew. He had a difficult relationship with Valberg. Valberg believed Finbar could not be immune to the gossip concerning his fondness for alcohol and hedonism. But Valberg hoped no-one really knew the gravity of his problems or the monster he could be.

Valberg's thoughts turned to the murders. Some of the victims' injuries had been horrific, but it was Majella McLaughlin's death that haunted him. The terror on her face, the rosary beads lying on the floor that she must have been clutching. It seemed the killer showed Majella some compassion. He did not cut her throat or torture her. Perhaps it was an act of mercy to send her to her death while praying. Why would anyone end an elderly woman's life this way?

Meanwhile, the media and politicians were in their own self-induced frenzy of speculation and condemnation. The inevitability of it all sickened Valberg. He realised, nonetheless, that he should not blame the media. They had a story to tell and they did not murder the victims.

Valberg felt he was missing something. What had these victims got in common? They were all harmless and defenceless. They were no threat to anyone. Who could have wanted them dead, and why?

He watched the Bogside and Creggan begin to stir, and from the Walls he saw a restless crowd milling around in Cable Street. As more residents and PSNI officers gathered at the scene, tension increased. So predictable. Valberg thought to himself, as he often did, what situation was ever made better by the arrival of more police?

Valberg stared at the spire of St Eugene's Cathedral in the distance and thought of Majella's pain as she died not expecting to leave the comfort of her religious sanctuary in such a cruel way. He looked out to his left over Long Tower Church, the oldest Catholic church in the area. Its name came from the monastic round tower that had once stood on the site. He was conscious that the sanctity and beauty of St Augustine's and the deep religious history of the Long Tower seemed in stark contrast to the evil unleashed by the brutal and demonic murders that had taken place in their shadow.

From nowhere, thoughts of his father came to him. Gustav Valberg took great joy in researching the heritage of his adopted city and always loved visiting the local historic churches. Valberg's heart ached as he remembered the last sensible phone conversation he had had with his dying father and the other tragic events that were indelibly linked to that occasion.

Gustav tried to say he was not sick, just tired. Maybe that was the truth. Maybe he had just given up. Valberg was angry like everyone else. He contributed to the general sense of discontent that seemed always to simmer over Derry. He knew he would never go fishing with his father again. That hurt him. It may have appeared a small thing to others but not to Valberg.

Valberg took that call when he was with Felicity White, her paralysed husband beside her in a wheelchair, dribbling. Felicity wiped his mouth now and again. Valberg had just captured Raymond Grimestone who had broken into the Whites' home the previous Christmas Eve.

As his wife and sixteen-year-old daughter Diana lay asleep, Gareth White thought he heard an unusual noise and went down the stairs to investigate, armed with his son's cricket bat. Grimestone was unplugging the DVD system from the flat-screen television in the living room, neatly arranging everything to walk out the front door. Gareth took no chances. One crack on the back of Grimestone's head and he was knocked out cold. Gareth lifted Grimestone up and tied him to a kitchen chair. The others in the house slept through it all.

As Gareth was about to call the police, Grimestone woke up, asked for a drink of water and began crying. He apologised and begged for forgiveness. He had promised his children a DVD system for Christmas and he was at a loss. He had used all the money his wife had given him on drink. The victim in him played on and on. Gareth took pity and tried to understand Grimestone's predicament. In an act of compassion and forgiveness, and in the spirit of the Christmas season, he untied him and allowed him to leave. Grimestone was grateful as he rubbed his wrists, took a glass of water and wiped the tears from his face. He thanked Gareth and left, saying, 'God bless you. Happy Christmas.'

It was the last happy Christmas for the Whites. The next night, Grimestone stood over Gareth and Felicity's bed. This time he was holding the cricket bat. Gareth woke; Grimestone hit him so hard over the head with the bat that it broke in two. Gareth bit through his tongue and it dangled out the side of his mouth. The blow damaged his spinal cord, paralysing him instantly. Grimestone had masking tape ready. He put it over Felicity's mouth and tied her hands behind her back and her neck to the bed. She could barely move, and if she did, she would strangle herself. Grimestone raped her while Gareth lay beside them, gurgling and motionless.

Grimestone's eyes lit up when Diana heard the commotion and walked into the room. Grimestone lunged for her. Felicity and Gareth listened in despair to their daughter's screams, which seemed to go on forever. When he was finished, Grimestone ripped the DVD system from the television and left. Valberg was the first police officer on the scene.

Instead of testifying for the prosecution at Grimestone's scheduled trial, Valberg wanted to abandon everything, go back to America and adopt a bohemian lifestyle on the West Coast. His father's weak voice was in his head when he visited the Whites recently. It kept saying: 'I'm not sick, just feeling tired.'

Valberg did not hate or despise all solicitors and barristers, just a large percentage of them. He became depressed many times with the standard of the prosecution's work. The Bar Council and the Law Society complained more than once to PSNI Headquarters about Valberg's behaviour and attitude towards their esteemed members. Valberg was concerned Grimestone's trial would be yet another disaster despite the probable leanings of the judge towards the prosecution.

He thought this was it, the end. He would deal with the White case and then leave for good. Run away and escape and do what he liked best: enjoying his own company and that of alcohol and beautiful foreign women. No ties and no obligations.

In his last moments of isolation, Valberg looked beyond St Eugene's spire towards County Donegal, lost in thoughts of his own future and his father now lying dying in the Foyle Hospice.

CHAPTER 11

When Linda, Finbar, Michael and Abigail presented themselves at the Double Bastion, Valberg was still staring out over Donegal, almost in a trance. Another jet plane painted the sky. He looked down at Free Derry Corner and Rossville Street and said to Finbar in an almost whisper, 'Swept away. Those people down there. They were swept away like voices in a hurricane. A hurricane of bullets.'

Finbar just nodded and glanced at the others.

Valberg gathered himself.

'Right, what do we have? What we *don't* have is the luxury of time and mature reflection. I've come to terms with that now. The golden period of the investigation is about to end. We need something. Anything.'

They stood in a circle, Valberg facing north down Grand Parade towards Walker's monument and the Apprentice Boys Memorial Hall.

'Abigail, anything more on Sharkey? Specifically his head?'

'We may have something.' She eyed her colleagues.

Valberg told her to speak freely. Any view or theory from anyone would be welcome.

Abigail looked around. 'I mentioned this earlier to DCI Valberg, we think Mr Sharkey may have bitten the murderer's hand as he was being decapitated. My initial look inside his mouth with the light here was inconclusive. I'm not sure if what's in there is human flesh or tiny particles of a glove of some sort. But it may also be just bits of dirt. And just one more thing ...'

Valberg almost grinned.

'Sorry for the gore, but his tongue's gone. So, detective, I think he bit his tongue off, too.'

Linda asked, 'How do you know he bit it off rather than it being cut out? And where is it?'

'Too messy. It's a worn phrase now, but everything about everything that I have examined has been done with military precision. His jaw may have locked in the decapitation struggle and he may have ground his way through his tongue as he tried to bite into his murderer's hand. We didn't find it at the scene so he either swallowed it ...'

Linda groaned.

'... or it was taken by the killer. I need to look in his stomach, or what's left of his throat, to be sure, but I can't open him up here.'

Everyone went silent as they absorbed this information.

'Any other marks?' Linda asked.

'Nothing obvious, apart from his heels where he scraped them against the grave slab. But I want to look more closely. I may find some further evidence of a struggle or his having been held down.'

'How did he get here without anyone seeing or noticing something?' asked Linda. 'How was he taken from the house?'

'There's a back lane there behind the houses,' Finbar answered. 'One of the neighbours told me the Provos used it to fire at Piggery Ridge, the old British Army camp there. RPG7s, automatic fire, the lot. Then they'd get away back down the lane. He could have been taken out that way.'

'Okay, Finbar, check it out later, talk to the neighbours, the usual stuff. Abigail, what about Avril Gibson? Anything new there?' asked Valberg.

'Sir, I have just been told a small portion of the left side of a ribcage was found in the grounds of the cathedral. Constable Bell spotted it, didn't you?'

'Yes, sir.'

'Stop the "sirs", everyone. Please,' Valberg said.

Valberg thought Constable Bell would feel uneasy calling him by his first name, but Valberg preferred it that way.

Abigail continued, 'One of my team has confirmed it is human with a small amount of flesh still on it. It must be the deceased's ... I expect tests will prove that.'

'The killer will be disappointed with that,' said Valberg.

'Vaporisation was the intention, I am sure, judging by the nature of the explosives,' said Abigail.

'That family has nothing to bury but a ribcage,' Finbar said.

Linda said, 'Over the last thirty years and more, some other families had even less.'

No-one disagreed.

'Anything on the hooks and ropes that were used to hang up Mrs McLaughlin and Billy Black?' asked Valberg.

'So far, nothing we can use,' Abigail responded.

Valberg put his hands on his head.

'I can't get a link. What the bloody hell is it? If we don't get something soon, we'll lose this and Belfast will take over. The Serious Crime Unit will step in and we are history. Listen, everyone, I don't want that. Worse still, we'll end up with one of those profile people following us. Jesus, the thought of that. A profiler following me around. Jesus.'

Valberg's attention was then distracted by a group of police officers and others approaching from the direction of St Augustine's Church.

'Here comes trouble,' Valberg murmured.

The Chief Constable of the PSNI, Seán Carlin, led a throng of noisy media reps up to Valberg and his team for what appeared to be an unannounced, impromptu press conference. Of course, it had all been carefully orchestrated. The Chief Constable did not even need to talk to Valberg in advance as he spewed out the same news-spin he and all his predecessors had had no choice but to spew out over many years.

But what moved Valberg was the sight of Deputy Chief Constable Anna Harte at the Chief Constable's side looking as uncomfortable as Valberg felt. Valberg believed that Anna Harte was the only woman on earth who could look beautiful in a PSNI uniform. It was no easy task. With laser precision, Valberg was firmly focussed on Anna. Everyone around noticed, especially Linda.

Valberg ignored the Chief Constable – now in full flight, praising Derry and its citizens – and gazed at Anna. He knew since his last row with her that until he apologised and made up, he would feel the loss of her in his life. He knew now was the time.

CHAPTER 12

'The only thing worse than a self-righteous, bible-bashing Prod is an altar-eating Castle Catholic who has bad teeth and gums.'

This was Gustav Valberg's view on Seán Ignatius Carlin when he was appointed Chief Constable of the PSNI.

'Watch him, son. Why didn't that nice woman get the job?'

Carlin was old style and got the nickname the 'Pope', as he was appointed on the same day as Cardinal Ratzinger had been elected Supreme Pontiff in 2005. His background was in Special Branch and other murky areas some media and nationalist politicians were suspicious of. He was good with the press and usually gave them what they wanted. Going walkabout with the journalists now around the town he loved so well was a typical Carlin tactic, but Valberg could see through it all and knew he was about to be dumped on.

Anna Harte was well aware of Valberg's views on the Chief Constable. Her friend looked tired, drawn and rough, all in black while the Chief Constable was immaculate and wore the whitest shirt any laundry could produce. Neither the Chief Constable nor Anna wore a protective vest.

Valberg, still hypnotised by Anna, could only hear the odd phrase from the Chief Constable as he warmly greeted him and his fellow officers. The media teams were having a field day. Valberg hated this. An official PSNI photographer from the Public Relations section was snapping everything. It was a clever move on the Chief Constable's part being photographed at the Memorial Hall and looking over the Bogside and up to Creggan, continually talking about the people 'of this great city'. Then he began all the old mantras. Valberg registered bits: 'Terrorists ... province ... Northern Ireland ... community ... these organisations have nothing to offer ... only bring us misery and heartache ... pursue them ... no stone will be left unturned ...'

Then he said something that really annoyed Valberg.

'Detective Chief Inspector Valberg is leading the investigation here and we can be proud of him, as he will bring the evil people involved in these despicable crimes to justice. Screaming to justice, as that is what they deserve.'

Valberg knew the killer blow was coming.

'I am going to make available to Inspector Valberg all the resources he and his team need, including officers from Headquarters. Detective Inspector Stuart Dickey and his team together with the Serious Crime Unit will be assisting the investigation here ...'

Public humiliation for a very private man. Nothing could be worse. Valberg had had enough.

Amanda Cleary of the *Derry Journal*, one of the welcome members of the press, watched it all. The Chief Constable's press team said he would take no questions. But they came like missiles regardless, and he deserved every one of them.

'Do you have any leads, Chief Constable?'

'Is this the start of a sectarian murder campaign?'

'Are you advising people to stay indoors?'

The Chief Constable was flustered but tried his best to offer some replies.

All this was new to Constable Bell. He was bewildered.

'Where's this all going, Finbar? I don't even know what I'm doing or supposed to do. But I just keep asking questions. Isn't that guy Montgomery tight with Dickey? I've heard stories about what they used to do in Special Branch. It's not for me to say, but my notes don't add up. Nothing makes sense. Nothing.'

'Be careful, Michael. Question everything. Just do your job. It's all any of us can do.'

'Aye, I suppose so.'

Constable Bell turned to leave. Finbar nudged him.

'Look. Valberg has taken Harte to one side. I wonder what's going on there?'

CHAPTER 13

Deputy Chief Constable Anna Harte had saved Valberg and his career on countless occasions, the last when it was alleged he had put a member of Traffic Branch in an arm lock so strong the officer passed out. For Valberg, Traffic Branch were the lowest of the low. He thought of all the cases he had to deal with and how under-resourced the police were and he loathed the behaviour of anyone connected with Traffic Branch. Traffic Branch knew this and they tortured him. They also knew he had issues with alcohol and followed him in the hope of catching him drink-driving again or drunk in charge of his car. They had come close many times. His last ban was for a year, and disqualification again would be a disaster. There was only so much Anna could do.

The last time Anna and Valberg met and had sex – and the usual row – was less than a month before. They argued about policing, politics and religion continually. Somehow, the dysfunctional relationship heightened the professional and sexual tension between them. Both enjoyed it. Anna had been divorced for five years and had two teenage children. She was infatuated with Valberg and wanted to love him, but her heart was in turmoil. Valberg, in turn, wanted a proper relationship with her. Anna, enveloped with religion all her adult life, had never had such a dangerous and physical relationship with any man. Her ex-husband was the first man she had had sex with, Valberg the second.

Neither wanted to be a saint, but with the media lurking, they had to be careful in their behaviour, publicly at least.

'Anna, our last words were in anger, and here we are again.'

'Jon. Jon. I can't talk now, there are too many people about.' She glanced over at the Chief Constable who had just finished addressing the media and was making his way to his car. 'I have to leave now. Call me and we can meet up and talk.' She looked him in the eyes. 'I have a strange feeling about all this.'

Amanda Cleary was watching what was supposed to be a private exchange while everyone else focused on the mêlée around the Pope Mobile. She saw Anna Harte touch Valberg's sleeve lightly as she departed and Amanda's instincts told her their relationship was more than just professional.

* * *

It did not take Valberg long to call. They met at their usual place later that evening – Anna's sister's unused apartment in a brand-new housing development in Eglinton on the outskirts of Derry. No-one, they believed, ever suspected they were there. When Valberg arrived they had no time for conversation. Their bodies collided like a car crash. It was violent and dangerous. In his passion he always simulated strangling Anna with one hand while gagging her with the other as he was afraid if she screamed the neighbours would call the police. It had happened once when they got a room in the Hilton in Belfast; Valberg explained it all away to the uniformed officers. This was a world away from the safe, dull and depressing marital sex Anna had known. Valberg called Anna different names during sex but mainly Carolina, especially when he climaxed.

Now, spent, they lay in silence for a while. Eventually Anna spoke.

'Be careful, Jon. I'm in the dark. As usual. Carlin's up to something. I don't know what but I sense he's worried. There is a nervousness about him I haven't seen before. Deputy Chief Constables are expendable. He doesn't like my closeness to you.'

'I'm leaving the police. And maybe Derry.'

'Jon, you're not going to start that again, are you?'

'Start what?'

'Oh, come on. For God's sake. Jon, you can't leave. And your father needs you.'

'I find it hard to listen to him now. The incoherent rambling is doing my head in.'

'Morphine, Jon. It's the morphine. Go to him. You need him more than you need me now. Go home and sleep for a while and then go see him. Go now.'

CHAPTER 14

Valberg was never going to sleep. He drove straight to the Foyle Hospice on Culmore Road to visit his father. Valberg's mother, Josephine, greeted him at the hospice and joined him to sit at his father's bedside. After a few moments silence his father noticed them.

'Won't be long now, son. I'm not sick or anything, just tired. Don't you worry. Where's that nice girl I met? Andrea, was it? Anna? Anna. That's it, Jon. I'm going a walk in the morning or maybe the afternoon. Me and your mother. Where is she? She called the day at all?'

Gustav Valberg started to cry. His wife stroked his head.

'What is it, son? I'm half a man now. Both legs gone. Can't see well today. Here, turn the TV on 'til I get the news. What's wrong, son? Do you want to go fishing in the morning? Patrick? Well, he's too young yet. Just you and me, Jon. We'll go out on the boat. No-one near us. I made us new flies and I'll sort the food out. Just me and you.'

This was killing Valberg even more. He was thinking he should have stayed where he was with Anna and then got drunk.

'You never gave us any bother at all. You and all your loud music. Where's Patrick? I let his hand go. It was only a second. It was me. Definitely my fault. A second. Where's Patrick? Is he here? My little boy. We had to leave. Did you ever forgive me? Letting your brother's hand go and coming here. Your mother couldn't rest. You were a child really, too. I let go his hand. It was just a second. A moment.'

The crying started again.

Valberg had heard it all before but he held his father's hand and comforted him as best he could. The death of his younger brother Patrick had happened decades before, but in his befuddled state of mind his father seemed to relive the accident on an almost daily basis.

Valberg could hear the local news from someone else's radio and the bulletins coming through about the Chief Constable in Derry. The case was all over the television as well. His father's voice picked up again.

'You know what it is to be an innocent man sent to the gallows? That boy was innocent. They wouldn't listen. None of them. I failed him, too. Let *his* hand go, too. To what? Where did he go? Your mother loves you, Jon. Like the mother of that boy. If I had been as good as Henry Fonda ... He was here you know. I've seen him. He's about.'

Valberg and his mother calmed Gustav down and soon he drifted off to sleep, thankfully carried away by the extra morphine which one of the nurses had administered on seeing his distress.

His mother decided to go home for a while to freshen up and Valberg was allowed to use a vacant bed in a room nearby to rest.

Soon Valberg was dreaming uneasily. But this time not of rats. Instead, he had visions of the Apprentice Boys parade around the Walls of Derry transformed into an Andalusian *Semana Santa* procession with thousands of drums as the *cofradias* marched together. The brotherhood had ardent support from everyone in Derry. All Valberg could hear was the legendary flamenco singer, Camaron de la Isla, singing his heart out: *Las Doce Acaban De Dar*.

As the dream went on, Camaron's voice got louder and more haunting. The blue-hooded members of the brotherhood took the place of the crimson-bedecked Apprentice Boys. The images came and went without a rat in sight and only the depth of Camaron's expression to fill the heavy air. Valberg could see himself trying to talk to him on Grand Parade to ask what he was singing so passionately about. But to no avail. The Spanish Civil War offered much more pain than Valberg could think of and, anxious not to open still-raw wounds, he took it that the brotherhood and Camaron wanted to move on and leave buried what was already buried deep. They all just wanted to leave the past in the past. Valberg was telling everyone that Camaron was still alive and that he was singing about compassion and forgiveness. Camaron whispered in Valberg's ear. Everything would be okay. Love and forgiveness would survive.

Valberg's exhaustion finally took over. His dreams faded to blackness and a deep sleep enveloped him.

* * *

All was quiet in Derry through Saturday night and Sunday. It was almost as if the murderer was waiting for Gustav Valberg to die. Despite the Chief Constable's eloquent clichés, the people of Derry knew his words were hollow. Both communities had suffered equally and both were unsure if these murders were sectarian or random. The city held its breath.

Valberg got all the rest he needed alongside his father. When he left him on Monday morning, he had no idea it would be the last time he would see him alive.

CHAPTER 15

'You are kidding me. Absolutely kidding me. A lecture? No way. Not in the middle of a multiple-murder investigation and my father fighting for his life. No way. I'm not going, Linda.'

'Jon, it's only one hour this morning. I got the short straw to tell you. You have to go. It's all this integration with the community stuff. We all have to do these courses and lectures. We have no choice. Look, we are updating all the information and evidence we have so far in the system. We need the time to do this anyway. It is so much work. We are nearly finished and Michael and Finbar haven't stopped.'

'Jesus Christ. Magee campus. One hour. Now at ten? Okay, I'll make it. And by the way, be careful what you put in there. Dickey and the boys will view it all from Belfast before they arrive.'

'Sorry, Jon. They're already here.'

He looked at Linda, shook his head and left.

The plan was to sign in at Magee and make a quick exit or sit at the back and stay quiet. It would give Valberg more time to think.

Someone was just leaving a space on Claremont Street near the campus, and Valberg reversed into it. He wanted to be able to make a quick getaway. He found the lecture hall and saw it held a mix of people from the legal profession and university students. He would do one hour, he thought, and be straight back at work. He signed in, got his lecture pack and took a seat as close as he could to the exit. The lecture was about to begin: 'Trial by Jury'. It was to deal with recent changes to the justice system and, in particular, the conduct of criminal trials.

Valberg ignored the introductory remarks. He wanted out as soon as he sat down. He was agitated and thought the exercise a waste of valuable police time.

The lecturer continued: 'These people would have no connection at all. Picked at random and representing all of us. Moreover, the defence and, in particular, the defendant, would have all the details of the jury: names, addresses and so forth.'

A student from the front row politely raised her hand. 'Do you mean the actual person in the dock would have all the contact details of the jury? Their full names and addresses?'

'Yes. In fact, the defence solicitors would have been given the full jury list, not just the ones picked. You see, they used to be able to object on certain grounds on behalf of their client, which I will come to later, but yes. If you ever sat on a jury a few years ago, before a change in the legislation took place, the defendant had all your details. The major change in this jurisdiction came about in 2007 with the introduction of the Justice and Security Northern Ireland Act. Peremptory challenges by a defendant were finally abolished here as a result of that legislation. As I said, he or she would lawfully have had the right to see the full jury list for their trial with all jurors' details.'

'What if he was convicted? What if the jury found him guilty?' the student asked.

'Yes. I know. He could pay you a visit when he got out of jail,' the lecturer joked.

The audience shifted nervously. Valberg froze. '*Blodigt* fucking *helvete*,' he uttered aloud. 'Christ, I have to go,' he protested as he bundled his notes and jumped up.

The lecturer had a private list of the few members of the PSNI at the lecture and knew Valberg by sight. He stopped talking as Valberg hurried out of the room.

Valberg ran out of the building, calling the operations room at Strand Road from his mobile on the move. Finbar answered while Linda and Michael looked on as they went over details with Abigail on the secure files opened up for the murders.

'Finbar, get all the names of those murdered so far to the Court Service. It is a matter of life and death for the other jurors. Finbar. Do it now. Do it!'

'The other what?'

'Jurors. Twelve people picked at random. Headquarters should have their details, too. The victims must have been on a jury years ago. It's the link. It has to be. Jesus Christ. Jesus bloody Christ. My car is blocked in. I'll get back as quick as I can. Do it now, Finbar. Time is of the essence. I'm on my way. Jesus. Fuckin' fuck.'

Valberg began running as fast as he could up Northland Road, trying not to look as if he had committed some crime himself.

By the time Valberg reached the top of Clarence Avenue he was breathing hard. He was about to turn the corner when Finbar rang him, his voice trembling. Valberg stopped. It gave him the chance to get his breath as well.

'We have to come and get you wherever you are,' Finbar said. 'Stay put. We just emailed the names there to the Court Service and Headquarters and the PPS. The names are all linked for sure. DI Dickey got me into Headquarters and our own information is even quicker. I'm just reading it now. Let me see. Let me see.

'Regina V Gerard O'Driscoll, a Bill of Indictment from nineteen eighty-two, found guilty by majority verdict eleven to one. Life imprisonment for murder of nine-year-old child. Let me see. Yes. All four victims so far on that jury. And the rest. Just reading here. Oh, my God! Jon. Jon.'

'What is it, Finbar?'

'One of the jurors. It has to be. The address is right and the name.'

'Yes. What is it?'

'Your father, Jon. He was one of the jurors. Billy Black was the foreman.'

Valberg dropped down on his hunkers in disbelief. His world was spinning as fire engines left the station opposite him, sirens blaring. This could not get any worse. What type of death would his father meet? Surely someone would call the hospice and warn them.

Finbar was shouting down the phone as Valberg tried to get up slowly without getting a dizzy spell.

'Are you there? Jon? Sir? Are you there?'

'Yes, Finbar. Top of Clarence Avenue.'

'Sir, Linda is already on to your mother and the hospice. Police are on their way. I'm coming for you.'

Valberg, still out of breath, his heart pumping and his mind racing, shouted, 'Hurry, Finbar. Hurry, please. I'm on my way. Hurry.'

Valberg ran on adrenalin and fear towards Strand Road. Finbar almost drove into him at the bottom of Lawrence Hill. Valberg took the wheel and drove like a maniac to the hospice, the siren blaring. He nearly collided with a number of vehicles en route down the Strand Road towards Culmore Road.

Valberg sped into the hospice car park and jumped out. As uniformed police looked on, Valberg ran into the building. He dreaded what he was about to hear and see.

His mother and Father Doherty were standing by his father's still body. His mother hugged him and the priest spoke quietly.

'He died peacefully, Jon. With your mother by his side. It was a relief for him in the end. He asked for you and Patrick and said the boy was innocent. He kept repeating that and that you would know what to do. May he rest in peace. He deserves that.'

Valberg was heartbroken but relieved his father had not met the same fate as the other jurors. He felt guilty about having no faith and sad that he could not let his emotions out. The death of his father was not a great shock. Valberg had come to terms with it long before it happened. He was privately ashamed he had grown weary of his father rambling about his brother Patrick. Valberg had become hardened in his personal life as well as his professional life. The recent murders and the pressure he was under took up most of his thoughts.

As he stood over his dead father, he noticed a brand-new copy of *Human Chain* by Seamus Heaney. He asked his mother if she had got it for him.

'No, Jon, one of the nurses said some man left it in at reception with flowers and a cash donation the other day. When you were here sleeping. He said he knew you but not to disturb you. He didn't leave his name. Maybe it was a friend or one of your work associates?'

Valberg looked at his mother.

'Right, it probably was. I'll ask later.'

Uncertainty clouded his eyes but he let it slip by. His father was dead. He could do nothing about that now. He had other lives to protect.

CHAPTER 16

Valberg was beginning to feel the strain now. He wondered if his colleagues were wise enough to realise that Dickey and his cohorts were just stain removers in the classic style of the old RUC. If a case needed burial or distortion in the media, they would do it. They were fishing as well, and that was clear from their behaviour at Strand Road. He knew he had to talk to Linda and Michael about Dickey and Montgomery but his priority was getting the other jurors to safety, however many of them may be still alive or wherever they were after all this time.

Valberg phoned Linda at Strand Road and ordered her and Michael to get onto it immediately before the media got wind of what was happening.

Valberg asked if Dickey was in the room. Linda confirmed he was.

'The media will know soon, then. Go now. Act fast,' Valberg urged. 'You know what to do. Get those people to safety. But get me the details of all of them first.'

* * *

They were too late for Sammy Carson. His body was found lying in the ruins of Boom Hall close to the Foyle Bridge and the Foyle Hospice. Carson had been a keen fly fisherman and was known to be away from home for days at a time. He was a widower and his two children had emigrated. Abigail said Carson had been killed the day before. He bled to death, his hands and feet removed and left neatly at his side. Blood splattered the corpse and the rubble that was his death bed.

A cold, isolated, horrific end to an ordinary life.

Valberg knew the killer had been within striking distance of his father. But that was not a worry now. His father was beyond any further pain.

He knew something of the history of Boom Hall from his father, who had completed some research into the building and the importance of the site during siege times. Gustav used to get animated and interested in a topic. He would research it and become immersed in it and a complete expert. Boom Hall had been one of Gustav's topics. Valberg always wanted to visit but had no reason. Now he had a reason but no time.

Valberg thought of the young girl who was supposed to haunt the old building. Another great witness, he thought. The story Valberg's father once told him was that the girl was supposed to have been burnt to ashes in a locked room in the house. Sammy had her and the rats for company.

It was just as well Valberg did not go to the scene immediately. Rats were everywhere and already had eaten away at Sammy's hands and feet. His face was covered in bites and the rats had started on his eyes. Sammy's blood had come out in gushes to quench the rats' demonic thirst. The trail of blood from his severed appendages was lined with claw marks. The rats probably sensed a hint of fish from Sammy, too. Enough to make them frenzied. It was a disgusting sight and sent some of the young officers fleeing to vomit.

Linda and Abigail took charge at Boom Hall while Michael and Finbar made their way to a car park near the River Faughan where Carson's car had been found. The Faughan was several miles away from Boom Hall, on the outskirts of the city on the other side of the River Foyle, and was a favourite spot for local fishermen.

Finbar concluded that Carson must have been abducted from the riverbank, as his old bamboo-cane fly rod was found on the embankment. The area was closed off and became another crime scene, with white tents and platoons of forensic people milling about.

It was only Monday afternoon. Five former jury members murdered in three days. The media were now in meltdown, yet again. They were baying for blood, some were even reduced to what Valberg believed to be victim baiting. Family members were asked the usual insipid questions.

'What have you got to say to the people who did this?'

'What will you miss most about your father?'

'Can you tell our listeners a bit more about him? What was he like?'

'How do you feel today?'

'What have the police told you about how he died?'

'Would you want any other family to go through what you are going through?'

The last question was the most loaded. It touched on retaliation. Valberg despised it.

Politicians appeared everywhere. The inevitable continued. The newly formed Ulster Loyalist Army issued a chilling statement from their Central Command. Exactly, thought Valberg, what the Chief Constable and Dickey wanted. It said that they alone would defend the Protestant people and take whatever action was deemed appropriate to save the people of Ulster. The statement ended with 'God Save The Queen'. Nationalists in Derry viewed it as a pathetic attempt to create an excuse to murder Catholics.

Amid the wake and funeral arrangements, Valberg, lost without his favourite music in his car, listened to the news.

All the political experts were on the television and radio, confirming what their sources 'close to loyalism and republicanism' were telling them. All their sources lied, as they hadn't a clue what was happening but were too afraid to admit it.

* * *

The Valbergs from Uppsala and Malmo in Sweden flew in for Gustav's funeral which was set for the next day at noon. Gustav's will made his last wishes clear: where he was to be buried from, type of service and what was to be said at the church ceremony. The arrangements had been in place for some time. Long before the effects of his high dosage of morphine kicked in. They had to be followed to the letter.

Valberg verged on emotion when Anna, in plain clothes, visited the wake in his mother's house later in the day. But he did not break. They hugged and consoled each other, promising they would talk later. Valberg said very little to her. Anna knew him well enough to leave it at that. She would be at his side the next day.

CHAPTER 17

Rumours were gathering pace and Valberg was aware of them: the Troubles started in Derry and would end there; some maverick group was going to blow up the city; the PSNI were responsible for the murders. All this was adding to the panic and anger, even amid the days of funerals. But for now, Valberg had to distance himself from the mounting hysteria as he stood in his mother's large living room and stared at his father's corpse.

Valberg sought forgiveness and redemption. He thought of all the times he'd been angry as an adolescent. His only memories of himself were of constant withdrawal and anger, whether that was accurate or not. Moving from California was hard on him at such a delicate age. His mother was heartbroken after the accident. Valberg's father was losing her. She could not stay in Santa Monica or anywhere in America anymore. She tried, but it drained her. She eventually sought the solace of worship at St Eugene's Cathedral back in her home town of Derry. Valberg's father sought comfort in Seamus Heaney's poetry. It was the one thing that moved him.

Valberg turned to music and Canadian band Rush in particular. Listening to them play and exploring their lyrics allowed Valberg to think differently about everything in his formative years.

It was hard on father and son settling in Derry. It was easier for Valberg's mother in some ways, but father and son were always castaways. Gustav followed his wife and dared not have his son separated from his parents.

Valberg remembered the day he was accepted into the University of Kent at Canterbury to study philosophy and law. His father was so proud. Even then his parents accepted that he never would be a lawyer. Their son had made that clear.

Gustav did not convert to Catholicism. He did all else asked of him but not that. Instead, he took refuge in St Columb's Cathedral many times and got to know a lot of people there. The visits started when he found himself as a rate-paying member of the Derry public empanelled as a juror in the trial of Gerard O'Driscoll. He hoped the defence would object to him. As it turned out, the defence solicitors should have objected to everyone else.

With twelve Valbergs, O'Driscoll would have been acquitted. Every day Gustav sat reading *Death of a Naturalist* in the jury room on breaks to avoid talking to the other jurors about anything but the case. He'd take it to St Columb's Cathedral, just behind the Courthouse, and read it inside the church or on the grounds. He read it then, and he'd re-read it the rest of his life.

After all the family's friends and neighbours had left the wake house, Valberg stood over his father again and asked his mother, 'Did he ever talk about the trial of that boy?'

Valberg's mother sighed. She had brought her husband back to Derry. If not for the accident, none of this would have happened. The slightest ease of the grip of a child's small, delicate, innocent hand had led to all this, a sequence of events hard to contemplate. She let out a breath and sat down.

'I'm tired, Jon. Your father never wanted you to know or for me to talk about it. He took everything in his stride. His own stride. Just like you. You listen to no-one and care little for the thoughts of others, but there is a kindness in you that I admire. Just like in your father. He knew you well. He knew to leave you alone and you would come out of those difficult years. You were his universe. He knew this moment would come. And yes, he took an oath, but he was very upset when that boy was convicted. He cried. He had only cried once before. He kept it all in as you do now. Just like him. He even went to the funeral of the boy's mother. She committed suicide. Cut her wrists. Awful. Her home was attacked. Graffiti all over it, shameful treatment. Can you imagine what it was like for a single mother of a teenage boy convicted of murdering a nine-year-old girl? It does not bear thinking about. She had no support. Nothing. She couldn't even get to the prison. No-one would take her. She was treated like a leper. With no-one to console or help her, she cried ferociously in that courtroom, screaming at the jury, at your father, as that man Billy Black laughed at her. Black's actions meant the jury in effect convicted two people – the boy and his mother. Your father was disgusted with him and the other jury members.'

'Did Dad ever contact the other jurors or have anything to do with them afterwards?'

'Most of them sought your father out. Some died or emigrated. Mrs McLaughlin could hardly look at me. I used to see her at Mass. We developed a convenient way to ignore each other. She spoke to me once. Said that she sought forgiveness every day for convicting the boy. It destroyed her, too. She said hell would be too good for her.'

'But she did convict him … with the others.'

'Well, now you know. I swore to him in memory of little Patrick that I would never tell you this until he was gone. I didn't listen to the news or read the papers much these last few days, but when I heard Majella McLaughlin's name, I was relieved your father had died. The truth could come out. Your father had no idea what was going on. The morphine destroyed him.'

Valberg was solid as stone, staring at his father's coffin, taking all this in. He thought about the other jurors and what they may have gone through if they had a change of heart. He did not want to stop the flow of his mother's thought but he asked if his father had ever done anything else.

'I tried to stop him, but your father went to see the boy … or tried. He had vanished. Completely vanished. Your father tried everything. Every door he tried to open was closed in his face. There was no appeal of the conviction. Funny, but the main reason your father did not mind your joining the police was that he thought you could protect him from the boy, as a man, when he was released from his life sentence. He even went to the boy's solicitors, Sidney Rankin & Son, but they were very rude and unprofessional to your father. He was lectured about client privilege and other things. Can you imagine a proud man like your father being spoken to like that by that horrible little man Sidney Rankin? Your father even believed he was somehow involved in the boy's disappearance. Mr Haslette, your dad's solicitor, had no success with them either. He was like your father, old-school civility. The solicitors' representation of the boy was atrocious. It was disgusting, and they are still in business, claiming they are defending human rights. What a joke. You know, your father once said the boy was convicted because the jury hated the defence lawyers, particularly the solicitors. Hated their behaviour and their lack of attention to detail, something your father could never forgive in his work as a tax consultant. He said the jury members complained about their shoddy, arrogant, unprepared attitude every day. What made it worse was that the prosecution barristers and clerks were not much better. They didn't even send solicitors to the trial – as your father discovered later. Just streams of middle-aged women moved to the prosecution office to take notes at trials, prancing about with the weight of their own importance. And that little man Rankin is still around but he should be well-enough retired by now.'

'Strange. I sensed a strain between Dad and Mr Haslette. I never thought about it but now I remember those raised voices. It must have been over this.'

'Jon, Mr Haslette left an envelope in with me, he said it was to be only opened by you. It's in the hallway. Stay with your father this last night. You know that's what he wanted. Just you and him. I'm tired. I have to go to bed. I have had enough of everything now. Even religion.'

Valberg embraced his mother and helped her to bed. He was still emotionless.

CHAPTER 18

A bulky brown A3 envelope with an official-looking red wax seal lay on the small hall table. Valberg carried it into the living room where his father's coffin lay and carefully prised it apart as he sat down at a large mahogany desk. He removed a thick folder and a typed letter which he began to read:

Dear Jon

Your father instructed me to ensure that, in the event of his death, you were to receive the attached documents in confidence. I herewith comply with his instructions and provide what is known as *Donatio Mortis Causa*. It is a gift by reason of death.

I am proud to tell you that your father was my friend and I will miss him so very much. He was a principled and sincere man who had a gentle demeanour and a kind word for everyone in need.

Please accept my condolences.

Kind regards and my deep sympathy.

Yours sincerely
Ian Peter Haslette
Solicitor

Valberg spread the contents of the folder onto the desk. He was intrigued to find ageing press cuttings and articles about the trial of Gerard O'Driscoll, and the suicide of his mother, Bernadette. Most interesting was a collection of his father's own notes he had made throughout the trial. The jurors were not allowed to remove anything from the courtrooms relating to the case but this did not deter Gustav. Included with the bundle was his own battered copy of *Death of a Naturalist*, covered in observations, queries and diagrams. The jury keepers and the trial judge let him keep it with him, not realising what he was using it for. This was the edition he clung to after Patrick's death and took with him everywhere.

Valberg finally smiled amid the misery and his father lying dead beside him. He went to the coffin and leaned over, kissed him and put his hand on his.

As he read well into the early hours of the morning, the curse of the mobile phone struck, but Valberg was pleased, whatever the news was going to be, that it was a conscientious colleague calling.

'Finbar.'

'Yes, sir. I am sorry for calling at this time, but we've tracked down all the other jurors. You said you wanted to know and thankfully ... well, you know what I mean. Five have died of natural causes. Three of those had emigrated to New Zealand and Australia. It just took a bit longer getting consular confirmation and help from the local police and their families there, but we worked at it all day and it's all one hundred per cent. We have got the death certificates for them all now and all scanned into the system. That just leaves—'

'The last juror. Who is it?'

'The Sinn Féin guy. Eoin McFlynn. The councillor.'

Valberg thought it incredible that a 'Shinner' had voted to convict someone on the basis of evidence supplied by the RUC. But Valberg knew that the Sinn Féin councillor was closer to the PSNI than he would prefer to have his supporters know.

'Finbar, well done. Brilliant work. I want Linda to phone him now or call on him. At this time of night, it will be perfect.

I am sure you have patrols in place already?'

'Yes. Well, Linda knew to do that.'

'Right, okay. Tell Linda to give McFlynn my personal mobile number. Now listen. He will be nervous about not coming forward in the last few days, but it wouldn't have mattered anyway. Tell him to call me immediately and I'll tell him what to do. No-one else will know.'

'Aye. Okay.'

'That's it. He won't take police protection, so don't force it on him. But keep his house under surveillance night and day until the funeral is over tomorrow. My car ...'

'What?'

'No, sorry. Not important. My car is still up at Claremont Street. I'll get it tomorrow. Linda called around earlier to tell me about Mr Carson, although it has made the news. Not all the details, though. I couldn't leave here. I meant to give Linda the keys, but my mind was elsewhere. Mr Carson and my father. Sorry. I'm drifting a bit. Linda has been in touch with his son and daughter, and there were other relatives still in Derry. Were you down there at Boom Hall? I hear it was a terrible sight. What is this guy up to?'

'I dunno, sir. But ... look, I can get it for you, sure. Your car.'

'Thanks, Finbar. Maybe you can leave me up tomorrow. Get Linda to get on to the councillor now, okay? And thanks again, Finbar. Well done, all.'

'Goodnight, Jon.'

'Goodnight, Finbar. You're missing all your football and hurling this weather.'

'Ah, never worry about that, sir. It can wait. Goodnight.'

Valberg returned to his father's documents. McFlynn telephoned him fifteen minutes later.

CHAPTER 19

After speaking with the Sinn Féin councillor and more reading, Valberg was startled by the noise of a car outside. It was one o'clock in the morning.

It was the Pope arriving, unannounced, with security. The Pope, still in full Chief Constable uniform, apologised for the lateness of the call but said he knew someone in the Valberg house would be awake. After expressing his deep sorrow and offering condolences to Valberg, he stood over Gustav's coffin, praying to his own personal Jesus. Valberg wondered if his father were still alive would he think that the Pope was a complete hypocrite, too.

Valberg made them both some tea using his mother's best china. He stayed in the room where his father's body was laid out. One large candle burned. The room's most striking feature was the heavy, drawn red curtain behind the coffin. A Swedish flag was spread over the coffin lid, which stood upright. Valberg's father had requested that no religious artefacts be placed anywhere in the room on the one night he wanted for his wake. It upset Valberg's mother that he had made such a request, but she was prepared for it.

Valberg and the Pope sat together at the dark mahogany desk where Gustav Valberg had spent many hours working. They sipped their tea.

'We need people like you, Jon. How are you holding up? At least your dad is with the good Lord now, in peace.'

'I dream a lot about rats, Seán.'

'Rats?'

'Rats. Aye. I have not been sleeping well. It's awful. I try.

But once I lie down, my mind seems to turn on like a computer. Everything comes to me in digital flashes. Every case I'm involved in or have been involved in. Perhaps I have been suffering from the anticipation of Dad's death. I think he left us long ago. His mind, anyway. I found that real hard. It's difficult to listen to and watch someone you love so much, and who had a razor-sharp mind, crumbling physically and mentally. His confused rambling disturbed me. I am glad that's over.'

'Sure, Jon. I understand.'

'We all get very philosophical in these moments, don't we? Just lately, I have been reconsidering what we do and what we, or I, have done in my work. I have been overcome with a huge sense of injustice, perhaps all brought on with Dad being so ill. But, Seán, it is all-consuming. It's eating me. What have we really become? I think about this small island with so many unresolved murders. I don't want to add to that. We've created generations of victims. I really feel that way. I think we have contributed to the misery in a major way.'

'We have, Jon?'

'We have. We have contributed to it and should acknowledge it. Or we will have calls for public inquiries forever and ever. Victims and their families can't forget, and we or the State can't remember. It just goes on and on. Generational, as far as I can see. I've just been thinking about this a lot lately. I feel we have a responsibility. Is that a proper way to feel? Do you think so?'

'I dunno, Jon. Don't be so hard on yourself. We need people like you,' the Pope said for the second time. 'These terrorists want the war back. People like you. That's what we need. Law degree and a rapid rise through the ranks. You are a great credit to your father, Jon.'

'Did it ever go away, Seán? Even for us? The war? Or will it ever go away? Really? Ever?'

'Well, Jon, we can bring it to them. As a temporary measure, we could reintroduce—'

'You're not suggesting internment?'

'Why not? We get the politics and the law right this time.'

'But it was a disaster before. A complete failure. You can't just lift people off the streets.'

'Well, would you not want the terrorists who have killed all these innocent people put behind bars?'

'You mean these recent killings?'

'Yes.'

'But it's a loner. It's a one-man band. I don't think he has any help at all. None. I'm almost certain of that now.'

Valberg looked at his father and waited for the question the Pope had come to ask.

'I hear you got all the other jurors. Well done. Great work. And what of our friend McFlynn, the councillor?'

Valberg did not comment and instead asked the Pope if he wanted more tea. He refused, saying he would have to leave soon.

Valberg deflected the Pope's further views on the current case, disagreeing with him that paramilitary organisations were involved.

'No, why would they? The surreal dissidents have no interest in this, and loyalists? Naw. None of them. So, who would you intern? The informants we run? Just for show and a PR exercise? You'd need a whole legal appeal mechanism. Solicitors would love it. Bang goes conveyancing and along comes internment. Just what the legal profession needs now. Solicitors would be very grateful indeed. Because with internment you will get marching in the streets and civil disorder on a wide scale. Who profits from all that? Not the police or the public. We used and abused the legal system and, in particular, the judiciary the last time. It didn't take long for the judges to see through it all. And us. Internment and supergrass trials. You think that'll sort out this killing machine?'

'That's what I mean. We get it right this time. The process. We'll still get a lot off the streets.'

Valberg shook his head.

'To where? The prisons won't be able to cope. It'll be "back to the future" stuff, recruiting a load of malcontent ex-police people to act as security guards and set them up for assassination. It would be a mess. No, Seán. Terrible as it is, it is not the spark you need to justify imprisonment without trial. What has happened is atrocious, but not the atrocity you need. We have a loner in my opinion, operating with

78

military precision. Someone with a high degree of professional training. But not a paramilitary army.' He looked at the Pope.

'But what about O'Driscoll?'

Valberg finished his tea, sat back and looked over at his father.

'He appears to have vanished. My team can't find a trace of him anywhere. Perhaps some of your old friends in the prison service or Special Branch could help us, Seán? He was charged, convicted, incarcerated, and is now gone. Gone soon after his conviction without a trace. Even Father Doherty, you know him, he clams up when asked about him. Did you know his mother killed herself? He has no family. Nothing. We can't find anything. It's as if he never existed. O'Driscoll is a real mystery man. A chimera. A ghost. That makes him even more dangerous.'

'Well, I'm sure you have the right people on it, and my team and office will give you all the help and resources you need. So what of the councillor?'

'He's in a secure location with his wife. None of my team know where, only me. It's Judge Nicholson's old place, the Beech Hill. I told him to drive there and check in and not to move until I personally called him. I told him to park his car as far away as possible from the main building, but parking is tight enough there as you know. Some of his own are watching. I said that was okay and police would not interfere. He has my word on that. In the circumstances he was extremely compliant. PR-wise, if it were known we were helping in his protection or he assisting us with the case, it would make his difficult life even more difficult. Well, let's not beat about the bush. He can't be seen publicly to be helping us at all. For operational reasons that I am sure you are aware.'

'Excellent. The Beech Hill, then. He'll like it there. Do you know the history of the place? An Englishman called Alexander Skipton had it built originally, but he was shot dead the day before he was due to move in with his family. So long ago now, but awful. Very sad. All in the name of a piece of dirt. The usual in this part of the world. Then the place was burnt to the ground during the siege. There was the American Marines connection, too, during the war, and President

Clinton stayed there. And now a Sinn Féin councillor. Ironic, eh? Anyway, I won't interfere or intrude further, Jon. Best wishes to your mother. I hope we didn't wake her.'

The Pope's body language was all about leaving now. He had paid his respects and discovered what he needed to know.

With a shake of the hand and a pat on the shoulder, the Pope left with his security, driven away into the darkness while Valberg looked scornfully on.

He returned to his father and kept reading the gift left for him.

At around three o'clock he phoned Amanda Cleary. They spoke for over an hour.

CHAPTER 20

Valberg, dressed in a black suit and white shirt with Italian collar and black tie, gathered his thoughts and called to memory the words of Heaney's *Mid-Term Break*, the only poem his father wanted recited at his short funeral celebration at St Columb's Cathedral; the dean there had agreed to this many years before.

Everyone was nervous. Anna watched Valberg as he cleared his throat, looked at his mother and his father's coffin and, finally, at her. Valberg was acutely aware that his father's will was detailed and precise. It was all he expected from his father, who he believed had been a highly intelligent, hard-working man, though one who cared little for the work he did. As he got older, Valberg could see his father only thought of his career as a way to provide well for his family and enable him to travel the world. Valberg also knew his father had so much poetry to choose from. Instead of praising him posthumously, he just wanted his son to read these special verses to the gathering. More of a test for his son than anything.

The church was hushed, nervous and heavy with emotion. Valberg did not let himself or his father down. He looked out over the gathered mourners as he recited. The imagery was so evocative for Valberg. Father Doherty sat with his eyes closed, his head bowed, listening intently and nodding.

Afterwards, Valberg fell into Anna's arms. Linda, Michael and Finbar embraced him warmly. They all went with family members and friends to the city cemetery for the burial.

The Valberg family plot already held little Patrick who

had been exhumed from his grave in California and buried for the second time in Derry. Valberg's mother insisted on it. The process had been fraught with difficulties, practically and spiritually, and the memory of the little white coffin was more than she could take.

Valberg's mother gave in to her emotions and it all came out. Everyone gathered around her. Valberg held her close and momentarily retreated deeper into himself.

Anna's security people maintained a discreet, respectful distance. Anna told Valberg she was still staying at her sister's place and to come to her when he was ready. She would wait for him there.

'I'll get Mum settled, and I need to get my car. I'll see you later. There is one last thing I need to do for my father,' Valberg said as they embraced and kissed gently again.

Amanda Cleary was the only journalist in the cemetery that day. Valberg got his mother settled with other relatives in the back of the black funeral car that had brought them. Valberg reached under the front seat and removed the envelope his father had left for him. Amanda had been advised in their late-night phone conversation not to approach Valberg until he was ready. She was nervous.

Valberg's father had written him a note telling him jokingly to ignore the good advice his good friend Ian Haslette had given him over many years and which he always gave his son: *never* write or do anything in anger or emotion. Step back, sleep on it, and the position would be clearer the next day. Instead, Gustav had advised his son on this occasion to give all the notes and articles he had gathered on O'Driscoll to some reliable, trustworthy journalist who had earned his son's respect. He told him to do it when his emotions were running high in case he thought too much about it and lost his nerve.

Valberg beckoned Amanda to one side. She had no need to ask Valberg anything. They had talked enough on the phone. Valberg asked her if she had uncovered much.

'A lot on the Pope, and some material on Gerard O'Driscoll. I have it here for you. But it's difficult to verify any of it,' Amanda said. They swapped envelopes. 'Thank you, Jon. I will abide by your wishes. Trust me.'

'I do,' said Valberg. 'I have to.'

CHAPTER 21

In exchange for his father's court notes and papers in relation to the trial of Gerard O'Driscoll, Amanda Cleary had handed over all her own research papers on the Pope and O'Driscoll to Valberg. The exchange suited both of them. Valberg was amazed, and concerned, at the depth of the material the journalist had uncovered.

Safe in the knowledge that O'Driscoll was never going to sue, Amanda had even prepared an exclusive article for future publication, depending on what would become of the Pope. She trusted Valberg so much she included it with a note declaring that it was of no evidential weight and that her editor would probably never let it run in the paper, but her view was 'publish and be damned'.

Back in his mother's house, Valberg quickly read the draft article.

"RULE OF LAW"
By Amanda Cleary
Chief Crime Correspondent

The Force Research Unit (FRU) trained and created human killing machines, and Gerard O'Driscoll became its most prolific and accomplished operator in a short space of time. Despite, or perhaps because of, his deep reservoir of anger, O'Driscoll became an efficient killing apparatus for the British Army and later a mercenary and professional assassin used by many governments, but mainly the British and the Americans. They would, of course, deny his existence when it suited them.

Allegations circulated for years, and still do, that a force existed within the FRU – the way Special Branch, of whom current Chief Constable Seán Carlin of the PSNI had been a member, was thought of as a force within a force of the RUC. This led to a lack of legal accountability. It allowed politicians and senior police officers to deny its existence truthfully on oath. They were then free to be mendacious about whether they had heard anything about the existence of a secret killing unit.

This secret group within the FRU were known as the Cromwell Killers. They acted with impunity. They had no manual or code of ethics. They, and Gerard O'Driscoll in particular, had no moral compass. O'Driscoll did not need or want for one. The rule of law, even as a slippery concept, was meaningless to them. It did not apply. The Cromwell Killers answered to no-one. Their existence would be denied, and one of their architects was the current Chief Constable. He could not deny his past to his close associates, who kept him in check. It may also have been a deliberate move by the Policing Board, who appointed him to see how long he would last. Even though Seán Carlin was the only candidate for the job, it was widely accepted that the then Assistant Chief Constable Anna Harte was much more deserving.

The Chief Constable brazened his glorious career out in the hope his criminal role would never become public. In truth, he ended up well down the food chain of the Cromwell Killers for his own good. But his role in identifying recruits for his British paymasters was crucial, especially identifying someone vulnerable – like Gerard O'Driscoll.

O'Driscoll became the stuff of legend and dread. He was fearless and numb. He lost all human compassion and morality. His *nom de guerre* became the 'Saturn Killer'. He travelled the world as a ruthless assassin but he operated best on his own for the British Army in Ireland. He used to think of the people he killed as just more unresolved murders that would never be investigated properly.

That's where the Chief Constable, when he was a detective sergeant in Special Branch, came in again. He would oversee a deliberately shoddy investigation and ensure it remained that way. He became an expert at cover-up and distortion. He created generations of victims, and the only thing he feared more than hell was the Historical Enquiries Team. He hated it and more than once said publicly that everyone should stop looking at the past. That was easy for him to say while hundreds of families remained devastated at their loss and angry at the lack of justice they suffered.

* * *

The extent of this information made Valberg realise Amanda Cleary had even better sources within the police than he had. He thought such a brave piece of writing should be in the public domain. Valberg knew O'Driscoll would obviously not sue on the article if it were ever published. But he would not be happy about it. And Amanda might just be made to suffer as a result.

CHAPTER 22

'I'm Detective Sergeant Carlin, Gerard, but you can call me Seán.'

'Seán?'

'That's right. I'm your only friend now. I'm sorry about your mother. That's terrible. Really.'

It was July 1982. Gerard O'Driscoll was in no mood for pleasantries or civility. He was in jail for something he had not done and his mother had just committed suicide. He was refused compassionate bail to attend her funeral on the grounds of his own safety and outrageous cost to the public purse. He had nothing now.

'Gerard, we've started a new organisation you might be interested in. It's a sort of research unit. Now, I'm just a messenger. You'd be working for, or should I say, you would be trained by, a highly skilled unit of the army. Young men like you, fit and able, would be trained for a special unit within the organisation. The force needs people like you.'

'You want me to tout in here? Jesus Christ, are you a fucking moron? I'm in solitary confinement most of the time. Do you know how many death threats I've had already? And the type of death I am promised in here? For something I didn't fucking do!'

'No, Gerard. And there is no need to take the good Lord's name in vain, now, is there? Come on, son. We can make a life for you. You are dead in here and dead when you get out. We can train you and give you a chance. A better chance than your appeal has. We have taken care of that, too. The appeal will be lost. Your solicitor has been very helpful. You can just disappear. No-one will know. No-one visits or wants to visit you. You will have a new identity. A new you. A fresh start. Or stay here in solitary confinement until you die. The choice is yours, but this is a great offer. Someone from the army will give you a wee visit soon, son.'

'Hobson's choice, eh, Carlin? A fucker like you should know what that means. Is that your real name? Carlin? That fucking name came up somewhere. I'll ask Father Doherty. The force needs people like me? Are you a *Star Wars* fan or just an arsehole? Go fuck yourself. You Special Branch boys talk some shite. Fuck, you have Special Branch written all over ye. Bastard. Fuck off now. Bastard.'

'Now, now, Gerard. Come on, son. Would you not like to help yourself? There's nothing here for you. Is there, now? Look, forget about Father Doherty. He won't trouble you, either.'

'What do you fucking mean? He looked after me and me ma. More than that useless solicitor. Jesus, every time I think of him, my blood boils. What's wrong with Father Doherty? What did you fucking say about him?'

'Just a little complication for him. Nothing we can't help him with. He'll stick to his teaching, for the moment anyway. Then a wee trip to Africa or something like that. But he'll not be coming to see you again. Everyone you know will leave you in the end. Sad, really. I can see you're stunned. At least you've stopped cursing. Thank God for that.'

'Carlin, go fuck yourself.'

* * *

Gerard O'Driscoll had stumbled upon the body of nine-year-old Orla Harkin lying along the river embankment of the Letterkenny Road, 'out the line', as it was known. A railway line used to run from Derry to Donegal and beyond, but time and economics ended that. The tracks still remained, perhaps an expression of optimism.

Orla had disappeared the day before after going for a pint of milk from her home on the Lecky Road. Gerard had never seen a dead body before. It would be the first of many. When he spread his school blazer out on the grass to sit on and opened his book, he did not even notice Orla so close to him.

Something was eating at Gerard that day and he was determined to get it out of his system. He wanted peace and quiet on his own. The curse of being interested in books and reading followed Gerard even after school. He noticed, but did not acknowledge, the two elderly fishermen on a small boat on the river. Or even a poacher using the shelter of the covering trees, trying his luck without a permit. Nothing unusual in any of this, as Gerard went to the same spot every day the weather allowed him. His mother never worried. He would always be home in time for his tea. Gerard may have been close to his mother as a result of circumstances, but there was no doubting that they loved each other deeply.

Gerard was older than the others in his class, having missed a year at school as a result of his father's murder. He wanted to stay with his devastated mother and help her. His father, Paul, was killed along with two young Provisional IRA men whose bomb exploded prematurely as they carried it into a petrol station. The owner of the premises had momentarily left the counter and Gerard's father was waiting to pay for petrol. Paul O'Driscoll's coffin was closed. He was buried amid speculation that the Special Branch or the SAS had set the bomb off deliberately after keeping the two IRA men under surveillance for some time. They could easily have been arrested, it was claimed. This version of events was accepted without question. The bomb-maker's expertise was never called into doubt.

As the years went by, a complicated situation got more complicated. The bomb-maker had been a double agent, and suspicions about him surfaced after various botched operations. However, he got out of Derry just before he was caught and vanished, just as his many victims had.

Gerard had turned eighteen and had to repeat his upper-sixth year at St Columb's College. He was determined to get his A-Levels, do medicine at university and ultimately become a surgeon. He had insisted on doing a fourth A-Level and opted for English literature. His teacher constantly argued with him over his take on certain books and characters which contradicted the standard approach. But Gerard could not let it go. He believed he was an adult and his opinions were equally valid. He was in a beautiful period of his life and ready to blossom personally.

So was Orla Harkin.

Gerard had been thinking about his future on that fateful day as he saw the poacher land a small salmon. He stood and watched the man quickly remove the hook from the fish and clean the blood from his hands. The poacher knew he had to hide the evidence in case the bailiffs arrived. All this clandestine behaviour for a small fish, thought Gerard.

Less than six feet away from Gerard, Orla Harkin lay on her back, as if sleeping, her neck broken. Gerard lifted his blazer and turned away to leave for home and his tea. He would never make it or eat his mother's homemade cooking again. He stumbled over Orla. In shock, he let out a roar of anguish, slipped on the embankment and toppled onto the body, covering them both in evidence.

What made matters worse was that in his terror and fear, Gerard tried to run away. But by now the two men from the boat had come ashore. They grabbed Gerard and held him down while the poacher went to fetch the police. He would rather have gone to the IRA.

The evidence gathered only proved that Gerard had been there, not that he had killed Orla. But it was evidence enough for a timid jury on the unsubstantiated word of his two elderly captors and an illegal fisherman to convict him. His free school meals card and the small picture he carried everywhere of himself with his father were even shown to the jury as they had been found at the scene.

Gerard did not have to worry about his academic future anymore. His fate was sealed with Sidney Rankin's arrival as his solicitor. The police always requested Sid, the 'Sleeping Solicitor', when someone was arrested who did not have their own legal representation. Rankin was famous for dozing off and not caring about clients at the interview stage – or any stage. The police could always rely on him. Rankin wanted his clients charged, as that was the only way he could make money. Gerard was intelligent enough to have been able to explain what had happened but, under legal advice, he was directed to say 'no comment' to every question put to him. This went on for two days. The police loved it. The investigating officers were Stuart Dickey and Victor Montgomery. They laughed all the way to trial.

Gerard's fate was sealed further at trial when he again accepted Rankin's advice not to give evidence on his own behalf. Valberg's father shook his head in court when Rankin announced this to the trial judge – in the absence of Gerard's barrister, who was late arriving that particular morning. No-one could save Gerard. Not his mother or Father Doherty.

Immediately after his conviction, Father Doherty pleaded with Gerard to change his legal representation and to base his appeal in part on the conduct of his own solicitor. But it was too late. The Pope had got to Gerard first, and Father Doherty let it all go after Gerard's mother committed suicide. He had received his own threat from the RUC and did nothing further.

This was Gerard O'Driscoll's introduction to the justice system and the rule of law.

CHAPTER 23

Finbar, Linda and Michael arrived at Valberg's family home to take him to Magee to collect his car. They had met with relatives of Sammy Carson and were on their way back to Strand Road. A meeting had been arranged later in the afternoon with Abigail Burns so she could give a more authoritative report on the murders. Carson's death had held her up, but she knew time was pressing. She also knew Valberg would be back in action as soon as the funeral was over.

'No more marching for Billy Bling, no charity work for Avril Gibson, no gardening for Paddy Sharkey, no more rosaries for Majella McLaughlin and no more fly fishing for Sammy Carson,' Valberg said as they drove off.

Finbar told everyone about a girl who had arrived at the police station the day before saying the 'Project Team' were monitoring her movements through an implant in her head. She said the world was going to end and everyone would combust in the next seven days.

'What did she want with the police?' Michael asked.

'She wanted a criminal investigation into the matter at the highest level. She was strangely attractive.'

'How's that, "strangely"?'

'She had froth building up at the side of her mouth. A sign her medication perhaps on the wane. But lovely girl, I thought. I felt sorry for her.'

'Good man, Finbar,' Valberg said. 'What did you tell her?'

'Well, what could I? I took a statement of complaint and told her when she comes back to ask for Police Constable Michael Bell, our expert on the paranormal in the PSNI.'

Everyone laughed. 'That would be some notebook entry,' Michael said.

'It sure would. I think we might need your paranormal expertise in this case,' said Valberg.

'Paranormal Michael. It sort of sounds good, doesn't it?' said Finbar.

As they pulled in near the top of the Rock Road to let Valberg out, his mobile rang. He saw a young mother arguing with a child who refused to get back in his buggy. The mother struggled with the writhing boy and the buggy while trying to talk on a mobile phone. 'Stand still!' she shouted. 'Stand still! Take my hand now!'

Valberg sensed disaster, afraid the boy would run out on the road. He told his caller to hold on.

'Sure, give me the keys,' Finbar said. 'I'll go get the car. You take your call.'

'That would be great, Finbar. It's just over there. Good man.'

Valberg thanked his caller, said he would call back and hung up. Cars hurtled up and down Rock Road, so Valberg stepped out and stopped the traffic, much to the annoyance of motorists. The child held onto the buggy and stared at Valberg as he crossed the road. His mother, still on her phone, ignored Valberg.

Valberg was looking towards his car when Finbar turned the ignition on. The car exploded.

Valberg staggered back and let out a roar, unheard amid the noise of glass and flames and falling debris. Linda immediately phoned for back up. Valberg screamed with anger, pent-up emotion and grief. Oblivious to the danger, he ran to the car. The heat was intense and smoke and fumes filled the air. He tried to prise open the mangled car door but it would not budge. Michael ran to Valberg and tried to drag him away from the wreckage and the flames. But Valberg was heedless of his own safety and resisted; he had to get to Finbar. Michael was screaming at Valberg to get away. Valberg was shouting for Finbar and to Michael: 'Let go! Let me go!'

Michael wrestled Valberg to the ground but struggled to keep him there. They were enveloped in acrid smoke and flailed around in the debris as Valberg fought to regain his feet. Although exhausted and dizzy with the fumes, Michael managed to restrain Valberg long enough for four uniformed officers who had sped to the scene with the emergency services to help him. Valberg fought them all and sustained a blow to the head during the mêlée. Linda looked on in tears, calling Finbar's name.

What a mess, Valberg thought, on the edge of consciousness. Derry was in meltdown and now a police officer had been murdered. As he faded to black the rats came back.

An ambulance took Valberg and Michael to Altnagelvin Hospital in the Waterside. Valberg knew little of the journey, and Michael, now in shock, lapsed in and out of consciousness. Valberg was bleeding from his scalp and his left hand was burnt. A paramedic did all she could to help them both. Michael worried that he may have hurt Valberg as he tried to save him from himself. He remembered Finbar and started calling his name. The paramedic tried to calm him. Then Michael lost consciousness.

Linda was left to manage the crime scene. She called Strand Road Station and asked for assistance. Within minutes, DI Stuart Dickey arrived.

CHAPTER 24

When Valberg awoke the next morning in Altnagelvin Hospital, Anna was by his side. His left hand was bandaged and, luckily, the injury to his head that had knocked him unconscious was no more than a bump. He had a dreadful headache, though, and felt paralysed by the pain. He looked at Anna.

'Where's Michael? Is he alright?'

'He's fine, Jon. A bit battered and bruised but fine. He's outside in the corridor keeping an eye on things. He's a great young man.'

'Yes, he is. He was only trying to help. I shouldn't have put him at risk like that.' Valberg sighed. 'And Finbar? I suppose there was no way he survived?'

Anna just looked at him, her silence answering him better than words.

'It should have been me. I watched him. I sent him to his death. I helped that child with the ungrateful mother. I told Michael. She pretended to kill herself. It was her. The bomb made me remember. It was that girl, from years ago. She jumped in the sludge at the river. I knew I recognised her. That's why she ignored me. Finbar. Finbar. Please forgive me, Finbar. It's all my fault. Why?'

Valberg rolled over onto his right side and whispered to Anna, 'Get to Strand Road and wait there. Don't tell anyone where you're going. I know you have security with you, but if you can trust them, that's okay. You will know best. You may be in danger on this. Your association with me will go against you if it all goes wrong. Is McFlynn safe?'

'We assume so. We can't locate him but we are still looking. A bomb was found under his car parked at the Beech Hill Hotel, but the press don't know yet. It was well away from the main entrance. He checked in but didn't stay. Abigail contacted me and wanted me to tell you the bomb at the councillor's car was different from Mrs Gibson's. She said this was important and for you to know. Maybe the dissidents were involved?'

'Not the dissidents. They know nothing. This is well beyond them. It's been made to look like them. It will be the same with mine, I guarantee you. Not mine. Finbar's. What a waste.'

Valberg tried to shake his head. He wanted to tell Anna all he knew about the bomb in the councillor's car. He'd just got a call from one of his own sources in forensics confirming it before Finbar was killed.

'My favourite headache,' he said. 'Left side. Ah, Jesus.'

'Try and rest, Jon.'

'He's safe where I told him to go. The councillor,' Valberg said.

He groaned as he tried to adjust his pillow.

'Anna, I only told one person where the councillor was supposed to be. It was deliberate. It was the Chief, Anna. The Chief. Do you know what that could mean?'

Anna looked at Valberg for what seemed like an eternity. He wondered what was going through her head. Valberg knew she'd had her doubts about the Pope, as many had for a long time. Valberg was convinced that she, too, believed the Pope's appointment may have been the final clear-out of the old RUC.

'What am I to do? I am the one adrift and at sea. My public face is one thing, then in private ...' Anna shook her head.

'Every one of us, one way or another, is adrift and lost. None of this is your doing, Anna. I need to get you safe. There is so much to tell you, but either the most ruthless killer you can imagine in creation is walking the streets of Derry like an invisible man, untouchable, or the police have a killing machine, well-oiled and fully functional. Or worse. It could be both. You need to get police officers around you that you can trust.'

'That's not easy. It isn't a big pool.'

'This is self-preservation, Anna. I think we have an enemy within, or enemies within. And a demonic serial killer on the loose. It's not all politics, though. This is the work of evil. By some of those we know, Anna.'

'Jon. I need more. I need to know it all before I can decide what to do. Tell me. It seems we are all in danger here. For God's sake you're lucky to be still alive.'

'Lucky? How would you feel to be accused, or worse still, convicted of something you didn't do? Can you imagine what that would do to your head? We build cases around the obvious when the obvious is wrong. We make mistakes, but this fucking place — years of purposely inept work blamed on lack of time or resources. How many times will the Historical Enquiries Team criticise us for woefully inadequate and shambolic investigations? This country is littered with them. It's generational, never ending, and we are all to move on? What a joke.'

Anna remained silent.

'Gerard O'Driscoll. Nineteen eighty-two. Convicted by majority verdict of the murder and sexual assault of a nine-year-old girl. He was innocent. Totally fucking innocent. You know the Chief's friends, Dickey and Montgomery? They led the investigation, or should I say contrived the whole thing, and the Chief helped them. Montgomery let slip in the witness box that DS Carlin assisted in the so-called investigation, but no-one picked it up. My father revealed it all to me in death. His gift. O'Driscoll's moronic defence team slept through most of the trial, arrived late, and were unconcerned as to their client's fate. I think that was deliberate, too.'

Anna could not hold back any longer.

'You think Derry is laced with conspiracies? Try our headquarters. There have been stories of threats against the Chief Constable. Over and above the usual. Whatever the nature of the threat, even all the agents we have planted with dissident republicans and what's left of the loyalists can't help. A special security squad watch over him now. I'm sworn to secrecy on all that, of course. I see some sense in what you are saying but not all of it. So am I to accept this from you as the truth? The real truth. Or did you really hit your bloody head harder than you think? Come on, Jon.'

'It makes perfect sense, Anna. Are *we* killing the jurors or is O'Driscoll?'

'Oh, come on, Jon. Come on. For God's sake.'

'This guy vanished. We tried everything. I had ourselves and all sorts of people search for him. It's a complete blank. He was moved and used, and it's like he's back from the dead. A trained killer. Working for ... who the fuck knows now? He killed the jurors one by one. Slowly and horrifically and deliberately. He must have. Who else had a motive that linked them all together? He had their details from as long ago as the trial itself. There is no other connection. Then there's me and the councillor. How do you explain that? Who ordered that? Who knew where he was supposed to be staying apart from me? Think about it.'

'Do you realise what you are saying? You will be destroyed. The Pope is a dangerous man. He will finish you. This is no speeding offence or formal complaint from the Law Society or Bar Council. This is your worst nightmare. He's a dangerous man, Jon. You need to be sure. Really sure. He will destroy you.'

'Destroy? Fucking destroy? Are you kidding me? Look at me, for fuck's sake. I *am* destroyed. I'm an alcoholic one month and a recovering one the next. My head's hardboiled and I'm on the verge of a breakdown every day, liable to kill someone myself. I could do it, you know.'

'Do what?'

'Kill someone. I'm there. I'm devoid of faith and belief. If there is a hell, I'm for it.'

Anna stood back, shaking her head.

'Listen to you. You sound like a victim yourself. Whatever this place is, it's home. Okay, it's far from perfect. But you or I didn't create all of this. We have to sort it out, though. What do you want, Jon? Get off your moral high ground and come back to us. Come back to me. Why don't you just talk to me? Why does it take all this to get you to open up? No more drama, please. Whatever you think of me. Whatever you want to call me, the bottom line is I care deeply for you. Many do. Open your eyes. Wise up. Shake yourself. Don't get lost in remorse and bitterness. There's a Union flag flying out there. It means nothing to me. Nothing. It means less to you. This place is divided, over what? Colours and religion? All in the name of what? Enough blood. Enough killing. I'm sick of it, too. But, Jon, here I am again. It's the last time I tell you, and unfortunately in the worst circumstances. Get your fucking arse up and get on with it. Where's your stiff upper lip? Jesus Christ.'

'Who fucking tried to kill me? I mean ... Finbar ... I'm so sorry. Jesus, fuck. What fucking vermin did this?'

Valberg tried to get up. He was losing his composure. Just then there was a knock on the door. Michael ushered in a bearded cleaner with longish hair and thick black-rimmed glasses. Michael assured Anna that it was okay, he had already searched him. The cleaner apologised for interrupting and quickly replaced the bin bag in the small waste basket. Anna smiled and thanked him. Valberg ignored him and tried to gather himself.

The cleaner stood straight, looked at Anna and then Valberg and said, 'You're welcome. Have a good day.'

Anna nodded as the cleaner left and shut the door gently behind him.

CHAPTER 25

As Michael sat outside Valberg's room in the hospital, he recalled his interrogation by DI Dickey and DI Montgomery about Valberg the night of Gustav's wake. In particular, they wanted to know what Valberg had been talking about on Craigavon Bridge the morning he and Valberg had walked it together.

* * *

'Well, sir, I put most of it in my notebook so I could remember but I may have got some names wrong and that. I did my best, though.'

'Why don't you just answer the question, for fuck's sake, so we can get through this quicker, boy? Read your stupid fucking notes to us,' Montgomery demanded.

As Michael got his notebook out and searched for the right place, he knew he was in trouble. Not because he did anything wrong but because he was certain that what he was going to read was not what these two superior officers wanted to hear.

'He talked about rats a lot, sir, and the river embankment and couldn't understand why more wasn't made of it. We talked about music a lot, and he asked me what music I liked. I said U2 and Bruce Springsteen and Snow Patrol. He talked about ... Alex Lifeman, I think it is.'

Michael looked closer at his notes and apologised as Dickey and Montgomery looked at him in disgust.

'Let me see, Lifeboat ... Lifeman ... no, sorry, here it is, yes, aye. Lifeson. Alex Lifeson. He's the guitarist in the

Canadian rock band Rush. Well, he talked about him a bit. A lot, really. He said he played with passion and precision ... that Rush were the best—'

'Give me that fucking notebook, you idiot!'

Montgomery looked at Michael's notes with disgust, then threw the notebook back. Michael bent to retrieve it. Montgomery and Dickey walked away and Michael breathed a sigh of relief. Neither thanked him.

It is just great being in uniform, thought Michael. Just great.

He sat down, almost breathless from the meeting. He was proud of his notes and his notebook. He took great pride in recording everything properly. He was supposed to respect superior officers and so he continued to do that. He thought they were perhaps under a lot of pressure. Michael read over his notes again. Some things did not make sense, but he blamed himself for that.

CHAPTER 26

Valberg was getting restless in his hospital bed. He knew he would be under security as a result of the attempt on his life. Anna confirmed several uniformed officers were present in the hospital and no-one was allowed into Valberg's room without permission. Michael was under orders not to leave the hospital while Valberg was there.

'Where are my clothes and gun? I had the gun on me. I remember having it with me yesterday,' Valberg said.

Anna opened the drawer beside Valberg's bed just enough to show his gun, wallet and mobile phone and told Valberg his clothes were in the wardrobe opposite.

'Thanks. And thanks for being here for me. Now, go, Anna. Go back to Strand Road Station and stay there. Trust me.'

Anna hugged Valberg and kissed him.

'I will go if you promise to come over to the station yourself. Promise?'

'Okay, I will. I will go over. Don't worry. Please, go now, it's safer. The Chief Con is in danger, too. If you've not already done so, you need to shift him to the most secure location he can go to. I am sure he's well protected, but don't let him out in public, Anna. Send Michael in. But not right away. Tell him to give me five minutes or so to get ready.'

Michael stood as Anna left, but she told him to sit down and relax. She sat beside him while other police looked on. Michael was nervous. Anna told him he was a brave officer and that she was very proud of him. She suggested he take some time off and rest.

'Ma'am, I'd rather work through this, if that's okay. I want to help Detective Valberg. He has been very good to me. Is he alright, ma'am?'

'He's fine, Constable Bell. You take care now. He says you can go in. Give him five minutes.'

'Yes, ma'am. Five minutes it is.'

'Goodbye for now, Constable.'

Michael was getting to his feet again, but Anna told him to stay put and left. Her personal security people left with her.

Exactly five minutes later, Michael knocked on the door and went in.

Valberg was up, his back to him, just about to put on his shirt. Michael could see that Valberg was strong and fit. His superior had a skull tattooed on his right upper back. Michael asked if he needed help with his shirt. Valberg declined and carefully placed a set of silver cuff links decorated with a Swedish flag motif in his jacket pocket. They had been a present from his father some years before. His hand was still bandaged.

Valberg stretched as if getting ready for a fight.

'I'll loosen up once I get going and get this bandage off. Jesus, my head is sore. And, Michael, look at me. I am sorry. You saved my life. I am sorry that you had to fight with me. That was all my fault. And I am sorry Finbar lost his life when it should have been me.'

Michael was about to respond but thought better of it and kept quiet.

'You don't say much, do you, Michael?'

'In the space of less than a week, sir, I have realised the wisdom of that. I write a lot down, though.'

'Well, be careful with that, too.'

'Aye, I know that now as well.'

'Michael, I'm leaving here now. I'm going to get a taxi. Who's out there?'

'Do you remember the girl I spoke to on the bridge?'

'Blonde hair tied back and pretty if I recall.'

'Jennifer Hastings, sir. Her team has been on security duty, watching us watching you, it seems. She's not in charge but likes to know what's going on.'

'Okay, let's make sure we keep her right, then. You stay outside. I'm leaving on my own. But no-one is to know just yet.'

'Sir, what will I say?'

'Make it up. That's an order. Tell her I went to stretch my legs. And, Michael, Detectives Dickey and Montgomery will be here looking for me soon.'

'Those guys were asking me about you the other day. I didn't say anything much. I only told them about the music we talked about.'

'Good man, you're definitely learning.'

'Thank you, sir, but maybe sometime I could go over all my notes with you. Could I?'

'Of course, whenever you're ready. But not right now.'

'Okay, sir. Will do. Thanks.'

'Well done, Michael. You really are a saint.'

'Ah, don't know about that, sir. No way. Don't think my wee brother thinks that.'

'You have a little brother?'

'Well, not so little. He's seventeen now in July. We are close, though, sir. We fought a lot when we were younger. He didn't want me to join the police.'

'Why not?'

'Ah, I dunno, sir. He's young.'

'He's afraid for you. You should treasure that while you have it. He just cares for you, caught in this awful job in this dangerous place. You are a good man, Michael, not like the two detectives coming here. You know, Michael, Montgomery and some others should have taken their Patten money and left the service.'

'Aye, you're probably right about that, sir, and about a lot of other stuff. Just one more thing before you ... well ...'

Michael pulled out his notebook and studied it as he explained to Valberg.

'Well, before you hear about the hysteria in Derry and all, I know it's not related, but it's just all these names. I went back to the railway museum a few times, and that alcoholic guy started calling me again. By the way, my friend with the IT boys thinks they have some CCTV from our own sources. The night Mr Black was killed. I'll let you know about that. Sorry. Anyway, it was only when Dickey and Montgomery spoke to me together that I realised that the Montgomery the alcoholic guy was on about was DI Montgomery. "Swanky Frankie" as he is known, sir. He said Montgomery was on the bridge earlier in the day before Billy Black was hung there. Or was there before we all arrived and Black was hanging there. He was confused. He's very unreliable, but my belief, if I can say that, is that DI Montgomery was there before us looking at Mr Black from the same spot you were at. Frankie was out drinking from five or six in the morning. He would be a terrible witness, but I made a note of all he told me. With all that is going on, it'll hardly make the news, but Frankie has disappeared. I can't find him now. He said he roared up at DI Montgomery and called him various not-quite complimentary names. I'm still looking for him and about to get Foyle Search and Rescue out. If that's okay, sir?'

'Do that, Michael. That's good work. I fear for Frankie, though. Do your best. Thanks for that. Will you phone me about the CCTV stuff? Don't tell anyone.'

'Aye, sir. Marty says—'

'Who's Marty?'

'Sorry, sir. Marty Ferguson. He's a bit of an IT genius. He thinks our cameras in the Waterside were deliberately tampered with but says he should be able to sort it, as whoever did the tampering did not tamper well enough. We could get the arrival of Mr Black now. Maybe spot him coming down Duke Street heading for the town?'

'Well, we don't know. It could have been from Victoria Road as well to get to the lower deck.'

'Aye, I suppose so.'

'Anything else, then?'

'Well, let me see ... aye, about the CCTV around the Walls, sir. I checked the footage from City Management, the Memorial Hall guys and again our own feeds.'

'And?'

'Nothing, sir, at the moment ... but Marty's working away on that, too. Strange, isn't it? All potential CCTV coverage of the murders missing or tampered with or faulty? Some coincidence that, eh?'

'Some coincidence, for sure. Okay. Do your best to put my two friends off. And don't be worrying.'

Valberg checked his gun was loaded and put it away.

'Right, sir. There are just a few other notes ... but perhaps later.'

Valberg looked at Michael.

'Michael, you need to master the art of what *not* to record. It's not something you will ever be taught, but you must master it. My father's solicitor taught me.'

'Solicitor, sir?'

'Yes. And one of the better ones in Derry. As I said before, be careful what you write down in that notebook of yours. And be even more careful what you *don't* write down. You don't want some barrister trawling over your notes and reinterpreting them in front of a jury and you looking like a fool. This conversation, for example, don't make a note of it. It's complicated, but you'll get it, eventually. They won't teach this to your colleagues in that new Police Training School.'

'No, sir. They didn't teach it to us in the old one, either.'

Valberg finally smiled.

'Right, time for me to go. Go and talk to your friend Ms Hastings and make sure *her* notes are okay.'

Valberg slipped out of the room and Michael followed him. On his way to find Jennifer, he passed the tall bearded cleaner sweeping the corridor and greeted him with a friendly nod. Two lowly workers just clearing up somebody else's mess, thought Michael.

* * *

Michael tried to explain Valberg's disappearance to Constable Hastings but did not want to openly lie to her.

'Jesus, Michael. Can you imagine the trouble I am going to get into? My sergeant just went for a coffee and left me to monitor all movements. He'll kill me if he finds out I just let DCI Valberg walk out of here without letting him know.'

'Jenny. He's only gone for a stroll to stretch his legs. He'll be coming back. That's all you have to write down in your notebook.'

Annoyed, she let out a sigh and searched for her pen.

'A contemporaneous note, Jenny.'

'Jesus, Michael. Where are you getting your big words from? You've been around Valberg too much. Contemporaneous. How do you spell that?'

'Whatever way you want to.'

'For God's sake! Lighten up. It was a joke. What time are you off duty at?'

'That's a laugh for us, isn't it, Jenny? We're never off duty in this job.'

Michael had had a rough week. He was utterly confused. His concern for Jenny and the trouble she might get into was the least of his worries at the moment. Anyway, her notebook entry should save her. He was as confused now about Valberg as the first day he met him. If only he had not made that remark about the rope Billy Black had hung from and annoyed Valberg, his life would be a lot simpler at present.

CHAPTER 27

The bearded hospital cleaner followed Valberg and watched him get into a taxi at the rear of the building. He stood off to one side under an overhang and waited. Minutes later, Detectives Dickey and Montgomery sped into view in a high-powered Range Rover then slowed down, looking for a convenient parking spot. It looked like they were going to abandon their car in an area reserved for the elderly and ambulances but changed their mind. They headed for a reserved space next to the morgue instead. The cleaner followed them on foot and approached their vehicle just as they reversed into place. He tapped on the driver's window. Montgomery slid the glass down.

'Gentlemen, please. Have you no respect? You can't park here.'

'Says who, fuck face?' snarled Montgomery.

The cleaner smiled, grasped his beard with his left hand and tugged it clean from his face.

'Now, now, Victor. That's terrible language. The Pope wouldn't approve.'

'Jesus ...' Montgomery gasped.

'It's a real shame you two get to die so quickly. Kiss, kiss. Bye, bye.'

It was too late for the pair to draw their pistols. Gerard O'Driscoll took a quick step back, drew his own gun and fired two rounds in rapid succession into their heads, the shots muffled by a silencer. Small, clean entry wounds in the fronts of both heads, large exit wounds to the rear. O'Driscoll had modified his bullets, filing them down so they would disintegrate inside the target for maximum 'dum-dum' effect – and maximum injury.

Dickey and Montgomery died instantly, their bodies held upright by the seat belts. O'Driscoll watched the blood and brain matter pump from their heads, covering the two detectives and splattering the inside of the car. The blood dripped down the passenger windows like thick red rain. The dark pink tissue smouldered with a whiff of cordite. It slid down to the seats and onto the car floor.

When killing at close range, O'Driscoll always took a moment, if close enough, to inhale the odour of the cordite. He knew fragments of the deceased's skull would be mixed in with the blood and brain matter along with fragments of the bullets.

O'Driscoll would have liked to stand and watch for longer. Ideally, he would have tortured Dickey and Montgomery, keeping them alive in agony. Even though both were dead, he thought briefly of choking them. He wanted to touch them, but time would not allow this. Instead, he leaned in, moved both heads with the barrel of his gun and fired into each left eye socket sideways. The exploding bullets blew the skulls apart upon exiting. The real purpose was to ensure that the victims' faces were destroyed and that their coffins would remain closed at their wakes, just as O'Driscoll's own father's coffin had been. It was as close to torture as O'Driscoll could come in the circumstances.

Now O'Driscoll was bordering on recklessness, but he didn't care. He thought about his father and for the first time in his life sought forgiveness from him. The scene he left behind was like the murder of mafia members who had betrayed their own to the police or the FBI.

Then, as if nothing had happened, O'Driscoll walked slowly to a nearby dark blue van, removed his thick-rimmed black glasses and changed clothes. All this was captured on CCTV, including him leaving. He did not care. It was clear he wanted the executions of Dickey and Montgomery caught on camera.

CHAPTER 28

Valberg went to the city cemetery. He wanted some time alone there, quiet time, without friends and family. He switched off his phone and stood at his father's grave. A multitude of emotions and memories tumbled through his head. He reflected on many childhood days with his father and brother by the seaside. Random lines and phrases of his father's favourite poems came and went. Tears welled and slipped down his face. He dried them with his bandage. Time froze for Valberg then. Only his saddest and darkest thoughts existed.

The shouts of two young children arguing behind him brought Valberg back to reality. He got down on one knee and put his hand on the fresh clay that had yet to settle into the grave. He let it slip through his hands as he whispered his goodbyes and turned away, heading for the lower Lone Moor Road entrance to the cemetery.

By the time Valberg arrived on foot at the Strand Road Station operations room, the news had broken about the two murdered officers. Anna Harte was there and looked worried.

'Jon, where were you? We were trying to contact you. Is your phone off?'

Valberg muttered something about clearing his head and switched his phone on again.

'Jesus, Jon, this is getting really out of hand. Montgomery and Dickey murdered at the hospital. Did you see anything?'

'Nothing, it must have happened after I left. It's not good for the service or anyone, their families, too, certainly. But

I can't say it's a big surprise. "Live by the sword ..." and so on. Is Michael okay?'

'Yes, he reported in. Christ, what's going to happen next?'

As if in answer, an officer hurried into the operations room and told Anna they had received an anonymous call with no recognised code words warning that bombs had been placed on the two road bridges across the River Foyle. Patrols had confirmed the presence of a blue van abandoned at the top of the Foyle Bridge at its highest point facing the west bank of Derry and a large lorry that had been left on the top deck of Craigavon Bridge. The caller also claimed a device had been planted on the pedestrian Peace Bridge, which was still under construction, but nothing had been found there yet.

Valberg's mobile rang.

'Are you watching the news? I haven't seen all the channels yet. Turn on the television, Jon. Maybe you have it on there already in that great operations room you very slyly commandeered. I know you don't like the news, but have a look.'

'Who *is* this? Who *is* this? Is that you, O'Driscoll? No-one else has to die. Stop this, you fucker. Why are you killing these people?'

'Now, look here. You calm down, and I will call you back when you want to be civil.'

Valberg looked at Anna. As well as the news about Dickey and Montgomery, an unprecedented joint-statement was issued on behalf of all paramilitary groups, denying involvement in the recent murders. This and the bombs on the bridges put the media into frenzied overdrive.

Fears that the bombs would devastate the city spread rapidly and people began to flee in panic. The three constructions that were supposed to link the people of Derry were tearing them apart.

Valberg's phone rang again as he and Anna watched the news.

'You and Deputy Chief Constable Harte, who I believe is with you there, I want you both alone. Just the two of you at midnight tonight at the top of the Foyle Bridge. In the meantime, if the army try to touch anything, I will detonate the bombs. All of them. There will be huge loss of life.

Believe me. And not just from the high-grade explosives. Chemicals – all the way from the Middle East to the North West. Nasty stuff that you can't hide from. Trust me – I've seen it at work. Get Anna to sort that now. And I want a power outage at midnight all over Derry. She can organise that, too. Walk towards the Waterside from the west bank. If anyone follows you, the bombs will detonate. I mean that, whether by air, land or the river. Do not come armed or with any devices at all, or you will die and the bombs will detonate. Start walking at midnight. Don't be late.'

The line clicked off.

Valberg's instincts told him he had been talking to O'Driscoll and wondered why he was ordering him and Anna to come to the bridge. It didn't make sense to him.

The Pope was already in Strand Road Station and his security team had informed him of the murder of the two detectives and the bomb warnings. He stormed into the operations room and demanded to know everything that was going on. Valberg had no choice but to tell him.

The Pope immediately took command and ordered a mobile unit to be set up at Culmore roundabout. He had the British Army in place and demanded a complete evacuation of everyone within a mile of all three bridges. By now, stories were spreading of a 'dirty' device with nuclear waste attached and of dissident republicans linking up with al Qaeda. All of it was nonsense; even denials by dissident republicans did not work. Panic and hysteria gripped Derry. As residents tried to get out, the world's media were trying to get in. Some police thought it might not be a bad thing if the media were around when the bombs exploded. By the time a no-fly zone was ordered over Derry, most of the international networks had their pictures to send around the world. The media were not going to miss this. Derry was truly under siege. Hospitals, north and south of the border, were preparing for a major incident. By midnight, Derry would be a ghost town.

An intense debate began about whether the police should comply with the demands of a murderer holding the city to ransom. It developed in the media, too, as the inevitable leak to the press was made. It was considered reckless and unprofessional in the extreme for a Deputy Chief Constable of the PSNI to be involved directly in such a dangerous situation. There was no precedent for it.

The Pope called a meeting in the operations room later in the evening. He expressed his concerns about Valberg and Harte going to the bridge. The Pope had the final say, but Valberg cared for none of it.

'I'm going. Shoot me if you want on the way. In the back. But I'm going.'

He stared intently at the Pope.

'You do what you have to with your security people. All the faceless men you're good at surrounding yourself with, but you won't stop me. Do what you want. There is a reason why he wants us there, and I intend to find out.'

'Now, Jon. We have lost three officers already. We don't want to lose any more. And, Anna. For God's sake, why would you want to go? To what end?'

'Time is not on our side, Seán. We don't have time to think it all through. We only have time to act. If there is a possibility we can stop the bombs being detonated, then we should try, shouldn't we? We have a duty to protect the public and not stand idly by.'

'Anna, with respect, your naivety is breathtaking. This person has murdered without remorse. He is utter evil. He has just murdered two of my most senior officers. Apparently it's all captured on CCTV; we are waiting on it to come in for analysis. Do you think he cares about you? You are many things, Anna, but you're not a bomb-disposal expert.'

'He has no reason to kill her,' Valberg said. 'And you know it.'

'What do you mean by that?'

'If he wanted to kill Anna, he would have done so by now. That's if he killed everyone or tried to kill everyone so far.'

'Jon, you have been under a lot of pressure lately. Maybe too much,' the Pope said. 'Why don't you sit down and have a drink ...'

'Do what you want. You always do. I'm walking over the Foyle Bridge tonight. Try and stop me. We'll get to the truth of this somehow. The killing can't go on. He can kill me if he wants. I don't care.'

'Jon, Jon. In the name of God, why would you risk your life? For what? For what cause?'

Valberg had had enough.

'Is there anything I said you don't understand?'

'We could arrest you ... for your own safety. Do you know this person at all, Jon? Personally? Have you told us everything?'

'Listen to yourself. You're drowning. I'm going. Don't try and stop me.'

CHAPTER 29

The Pope sat at a desk in a small office in Strand Road Station on his own. He was worried. He knew Anna Harte was right: time was of the essence. They could arrange as much security as possible in the available time. With bombs waiting to explode, doing nothing was not an option. The Pope realised she was prepared to take the risks that had to be taken. He knew he had to back her publicly.

The situation was unprecedented. But what was not for the Pope was his past coming back to haunt him. The past always came back. No-one seemed immune, professionally or personally. The entire population seemed to live with ghost cells that would activate themselves when the need arose. The ghost cells would awaken the past whether welcomed or not, good or bad. Saturn had returned for the Pope with a vengeance.

Gerard O'Driscoll had told him he was coming for him, the jury members who convicted him and anyone who stood in his way. He told the Pope he was going to expose him for what he was and what he had done. His connection with the Force Research Unit would be revealed together with the names of all the young men he recruited for it and the Cromwell Killers. He would expose every case the Pope covered up and ensured would go nowhere. Most importantly, O'Driscoll would reveal the true circumstances of his father's death and his own conviction.

The Pope dared not tell Harte about his past. He already suspected Valberg was on to him and his murky history in the RUC. He could be sending them to their deaths, but perhaps that was God's will, he thought. It could be done in such a way that O'Driscoll would get the blame. O'Driscoll was expendable now.

The Pope also knew that Dickey and Montgomery were responsible for trying to kill Valberg with his blessing, but they had killed Callaghan instead. Then, in an even more amateurish mess, they tried to kill Councillor McFlynn. They thought O'Driscoll would not get him, as they believed he did not know where McFlynn was. They thought they could have all this blamed on O'Driscoll. Their arrogance and incompetence were staggering. Because they had got away with so much criminal activity for so many years in the RUC, they thought they were above the law and immune from its consequences. They thought they could lie their way out of everything – as they had done at numerous trials, including Gerard O'Driscoll's. But they were sloppy, lazy and too keen to protect the Pope.

O'Driscoll's professionalism far outweighed their amateur attempts. McFlynn knew enough about the Pope to keep himself safe for years, but the Pope would not hesitate to have him killed when the right time came.

Thoughts of his own death began to appeal to the Pope. He could not take the pain and torture much longer. Sooner or later, he would be exposed. He had been threatened before and brazened it out. But now he could see no chance of redemption. He was becoming desperate. Coherent thought was deserting him. His MBE and hopes of a knighthood were in tatters, his loyalty to Queen and country a sham. He was not much different now from the young men he recruited, and the thought was driving him to suicide. Such an act would leave financial and emotional debt behind him. His life assurance would be voided and his family emotionally ravaged. His last act of aggression would harm not only himself but those few left who cared for and loved him. But the possibility was completely logical to him now. His blood craved being spilt by his own hand. He gripped a sharp letter opener that lay on the desk in front of him and stared at it. But the coward in him was never far away and thoughts of incurring the disapproval of his beloved Church over suicide made him think again.

As the Pope sat anguishing over his predicament his mobile rang. In a strange way, O'Driscoll's call helped save him.

'Hobson's choice, Seán. You fucker. I'm going to rip your throat out. Don't worry if you're thinking of cutting it yourself. I'll do it for you. Slowly. Or blow your fucking head clean off. Any choice you want as long as it's death.'

'Look, now, Gerard.'

'Gerard. That's a name from long ago. I got a new name. A new identity. A new me. Remember all that crap? Don't try that bullshit with me, you fucking rat. How many times have we talked about all this now? I told you I was coming for you and your henchmen. But don't worry. My great trial was your downfall. If you had been on my jury, it would have been an easier death than the one you will endure when I get you. All the protection around you won't save you now. It's the end. The whole edifice is falling. The Pope's empire will crumble. Saturn's revenge. It's not just you, Seánie boy. You and your police, your justice system, your killing machines, all fucked. It will take more than a barrel of fat lawyers to sort all this out. There will be public inquiries in perpetuity with you represented posthumously by your next of kin. If you have any by the time I spray my justice around you. Justice and the rule of law? What a joke in this place. Justice? What does that mean, eh? Those cowardly bastards got their justice for sure. That Billy fat bastard Black smirking at my mother. I fucking swore then I'd track every last one of them down. You know he cried the most? Like a baby as he swung around his funeral parlour upside down, and made so much lighter with all his blood flowing out of him. Fat bastard. I made sure he died slowly. Really slowly, and he cried to the end. Fucking begging. I am telling you this so you can think about what I am going to do to you.'

The Pope had been on the receiving end of this type of call for weeks and had almost got used to it. He challenged O'Driscoll at first, trying to draw him out and arrange to meet so he could have him killed. So the Pope knew even now to keep his mouth shut. The Pope behaved like a seasoned solicitor who knew there was no point interrupting a deranged client on a roll, talking about their great case. He, Valberg and O'Driscoll were a trio, each in crisis in some

116

shape or form. The Pope was resigned to his fate. He knew now, with Dickey and Montgomery dead, that he was finished. O'Driscoll's final words to him were chilling.

'Years I've waited. From Derry to Belfast. Belfast to the Balkans. From the Balkans to Angola and beyond and back now to watch you squirm and die like a bleeding pig. I will have no mercy for you. I am free from my past and I'm going to make sure you have no future. I am your worst fucking nightmare. I learned to kill, for sure. I have you to thank for that. I never took pleasure in it. I only started to enjoy myself listening to some of those fucking jurors squeal for mercy. Begging for forgiveness and crying like children as they died slowly and painfully. I stared at them so I'd be the last thing they'd see. I made sure of that. I couldn't listen to that fucker Gibson and her put-on la-di-dah accent. I'd heard enough of that, so I incinerated her. Those fucking cowardly jurors. They remembered my innocent face, alright. The boy I was and the life you took away from me and my mother and father, you worm. You slime-dog. My only regret is having to kill Dickey and Montgomery so quickly. But needs must. Adapt or die. Deal with the situation. Do you know how long I thought about killing those two? Those bastards killed my father, with your blessing, to protect a fucking low-life miserable rat of a tout. You brought us a lifetime of misery. You fucking wretch low-life scumbag. I'm going to do to you what Goya had Saturn do, with Saturn devouring one of his own sons. I stood in the Prado in Madrid just recently, staring at that painting, dreaming about killing you. It was in preparation for coming here at the right time. My hands around your neck will be like Saturn's in that painting around the body of his son. I will grip you so hard. I intend to draw blood from your throat. With my bare hands. I will bite you until you die, you bastard.'

The Pope knew the painting O'Driscoll had mentioned. He could picture it clearly and he thought O'Driscoll must have gone completely mad. It was the only explanation for the obscene ranting and surreal references.

'Are you finished now? Because I am. Do what you want,' the Pope said.

O'Driscoll's insults and bloodthirsty threats made the

Pope more resilient. He put down the letter opener, wondering what he had been thinking.

The Pope hung up the phone and it immediately rang again. He answered it and had a brief but animated conversation with the head of his security team. He had just finished his call when Valberg and Anna entered.

'We're going now,' Valberg said.

'Of course you are. You have my full blessing and support. It seems the higher powers in my security team are getting concerned, so I am about to be moved to a secure location now. So good luck. Operational command is passed to Anna. Well, Anna, I think the Police Act of 2000 may save the day. Whatever you do, don't get those idiots on the Policing Board involved if you can avoid it. Take care. Good luck. Good luck to both of you. I never meant for this to be this way. You must believe me. Jon, Anna, do you understand? I had no choice. I just hope you can find a way to forgive me.'

The Pope called his security entourage in. They had been shadowing him everywhere recently.

* * *

The Pope was ushered away to safety like an American president. Valberg was disgusted. He wondered if he would ever see him alive again and if so, where and under what circumstances.

Part of Valberg wanted O'Driscoll to capture the Pope, to see him tortured and killed. Although clearly not lawful, it was how Valberg felt at that moment. But in reality, Valberg would probably be the first person to protect him. Even the devil had to have due process of law for Valberg.

Despite his unconventional approach to his job, Valberg had to practise the rule of law no matter what he thought of it. He was traditionalist and conservative when it came to the administration of justice. The PSNI had to work, and he was part of it. He had to be a policeman for all seasons and uphold the rule of law.

Valberg was angry at the Pope, even through the fear that was settling over him, but he could not reveal his emotions. Just at that moment he could hear in his head the distant voice of Janice Sloan, the young girl who had committed suicide in prison. Valberg believed he could see her walk in front of him, showing the self-mutilation from her wrists to her elbows. She held her arms up for all to see, but no-one noticed her apart from Valberg.

CHAPTER 30

Anna and Valberg had one hour to get to the Foyle Bridge. Valberg insisted Linda, Michael and Abigail come with them as back-up he could trust. They drove past the massed media ranks who had been kept well away from the bridge and who were complaining bitterly to anyone who would listen. No-one was listening.

The thought of walking towards a van bomb was terrifying to Valberg. Why would O'Driscoll want this? The most senior acting member of the PSNI in uniform was risking almost certain death with a maverick policeman, who seemed to have a death wish himself, by her side. It appeared utterly reckless and futile to Valberg.

Anna trusted Valberg. She had to, and she had to pretend she was not in terror. She had no chance to say goodbye to anyone as it approached midnight and the electrical power around most of Derry began to fade. All of a sudden she thought of the gold cross around her neck. She took it off at the command post occupied by police and army bomb-disposal teams at one of the lay-bys before the Foyle Bridge. Anna looked at the small Celtic cross with a tiny diamond in the centre. Her mother had given it to her. Anna's will bequeathed it and all her other jewellery and personal possessions to her daughter. She asked Linda to keep it safe for her.

Anna noticed Abigail Burns and her team. They usually turned up *after* a death, not before. She looked at them, imagining herself as another torn body at a crime scene, someone poking at her charred, smoking flesh and writing a report and taking photographs with a flash so brilliant it could almost wake the dead. She would be in another closed coffin and possibly identifiable only by her dental records.

In typical style, Valberg did not want to speak to anyone. A British soldier, trying to do his best, gave as much advice as he could about what to look out for around the van. What a waste of time. Valberg thought of the people who had committed suicide by jumping off the Foyle Bridge. What if he had to jump over? Would he? Would Anna? The impact would probably kill them anyway. Worse still, what if the tide were out and they landed on the ground below? Hitting concrete from such a height could make a body explode.

O'Driscoll had picked the location for the van deliberately. It would be difficult to see him from either side of the bridge if he were there. The theory discussed by the emergency services was that he must be hiding in the van. There was no way they could envisage him breaking the cordons around the bridge to get to the van and surviving. Valberg wanted him there. His sense was that after going to all this trouble, for O'Driscoll to then call him on a mobile phone in the van was too obvious and predictable. He had to be there. He just had to be.

Valberg reluctantly admired O'Driscoll's attention to detail. O'Driscoll must have scouted the area and checked every vantage point from which a sniper could possibly shoot him. He must have positioned the van where he did to minimise exposure to any attack. He must also have a plan to get away, or perhaps he was reckless by now. Perhaps he, too, had had enough. If he were to be vaporised, who would care?

Valberg's phone rang just as he was about to pass it to Michael.

'Are you ready, Jon? This is almost the end. You think of that now and keep calm. If you both do exactly as I say you will live. You know I want the new Chief Constable with you. All going to plan so far. I do not want to kill you, by the way. Either of you. But I will if I have to. Come on.'

Tension and fear grew. Everyone was quiet now, more out of respect for Anna and Valberg than anything else. Everyone was concerned for them, especially for Anna. She was the boss most of the police wanted, and to lose her this way would be such a waste. It seemed the whole world was watching.

Valberg gave his mobile phone to Michael and left it on.

'If he calls again, you answer it,' Valberg said, shrugging. He thought about his mother for a few seconds but quickly gathered himself again. If he was going to die, he thought, at least it would be with Anna.

Michael asked Valberg what the soldier had said to him.

'Duck and cover,' Valberg said. 'Or if I smell ammonium nitrate to run like fuck. Great advice. Oh, I've still got these. Here, you keep them for me.'

Valberg gave Michael the cuff links his father had given him with the Swedish flag on them.

'Let's do this, Anna. Let's go,' Valberg said.

Anna tried to be positive and remarked that they were well covered by teams of snipers, but Valberg thought it a waste of time.

'Bullets won't stop bombs,' he said under his breath as they set off. 'The distance to the van makes it awkward as well, especially in the dark and with the breeze over the river. He chose his spot well. It will take a superior marksman to get him ... or us.'

CHAPTER 31

Military and police marksmen using night-vision lenses were in place at every vantage point close to Foyle Bridge; the amount of firepower covering the area was enormous. There was a section of the bridge, however, almost no-one could see, and that's where the van was sitting – just where it dipped slightly at its highest point facing Culmore so only a few marksmen from that side of the river could draw a bead on it.

The PSNI were relaying live video of events on the bridge from their own cameras to the Pope in his secure location. O'Driscoll had once again knocked out all the CCTV systems in the area. It was one of the easiest missions he had ever participated in. His training, expertise and years of experience as a killing machine protected him now.

'What are we doing, Jon, walking into the darkness?'

'You don't doubt me now, do you? Not now. Stay close to me. If he is here he will be in control. We don't have a choice. Keep walking. Do as he says if he's here.'

'This thing could explode. We are walking straight towards a bomb.'

'Anna, now is not the time.'

'Now that I'm doing this I can see it's insane.'

'Are you testing me or are you serious? Jesus Christ. Let it go.'

'Are we going to be the subject of this new Presumption of Death Act?'

'Anna, sweet fuck. Let it go.'

'We won't even have your friend Abigail poking at us. Nothing will be left to poke at.'

'Anna, please. We have both been through enough.'

'What will we do when we get there?'

'Anna, everything we have been trained to do is useless. We need to become formless and adapt. He doesn't want to kill us. He could have killed my father any time. Or us. He's gone in the head. Completely broken down. But he's so precise in what he's done. He's playing with us. This is all drama. It's all about power. He has it now, so we will do what he says. Remember, he was convicted almost thirty years ago for something he didn't do and then vanished. I have a feeling about where he ended up but maybe I can confirm it with him. Stay calm and focused. Bluff your way. Sure we all do it. You know we have a responsibility here. We convicted him. We need to put this right.'

Anna sighed and shook her head.

They walked the rest of the way in silence and saw the outline of the van as they got closer on the incline.

Anna spoke more softly now. 'I thought I saw something. At the side of the van, Jon. Can you see?'

'No, Anna, I can see nothing yet. Keep walking, we're nearly there.'

CHAPTER 32

Valberg and Anna slowed. They squinted at the van.
Fear flooded their bodies and filled their minds. Anna
thought about Avril Gibson and all that was left of her. A
small piece of flesh dangling on a small piece of her ribcage.
She thought again about Abigail Burns poking at her lifeless and simmering torso.

They looked at each other, not knowing if their next move
or breath would be their last. Then a voice from the darkness.

'That's far enough. Do as I say now. Stop. Turn around,
put your hands on the back of your heads. Kneel, facing Culmore. Do it now, quickly. We have some time. Not much,
regrettably. The lights from the van will come on. They're
very bright. Down now. That's it. Well done. Welcome to the
Nemesis Project. It's coming to a head now ... But later with
that ... if we get the time.'

The lights came on full beam. O'Driscoll became a huge
shadow which revealed he had some type of a stocky weapon
trained on them.

'Right, that's it. The clock is ticking. If you look around,
sideways, up or down, you will die. A quick shot to your
head. You won't feel a thing. A quick pop, then nothing-
ness. Blackness and the devil. Am I talking too much? Living in a jungle in Angola for months on end or watching
the slaughter at Srebrenica sort of affects your thought
processes. You tend to ramble. Setting bombs off here and
killing people on orders mixes your morality up. Just a little. So there we are.'

Valberg steeled himself. 'Why did you kill those people? If I'm going to die here, I want to know. Why?'

'I watched and protected your father, Jonny boy. I ...' O'Driscoll took a few steps closer. He rubbed the left side of his face on the weapon he had trained on Valberg and Anna. His voice became even more commanding. 'I never touched that girl. I didn't kill her. It's haunted me all my life. It's shaped the killer I am. You know that. Everyone paid for it. Everyone burned. I am not so proud I can't admit my murderous past. According to Matthew, Jesus said "solemnly" that tax collectors and prostitutes are making their way into the Kingdom of God. I am sure we can add bankers to that list, and if that's the case, even you and me, Jon. Faith is hard, Jon.'

'Are you the Saturn Killer? Did you kill all those elderly people here? How many other innocent victims are you responsible for?'

'For Queen and country, pleasure or revenge? Remember, Jon, the King, or in my case the Queen, can do no wrong.'

'Gerard, this has to stop.'

'Are you joking? I've only started. I'm saving the best for later. But it has to stop, for sure. I'm going to get as much done as possible before Saturn moves again. But I can tell you I'm also ready to make a mistake and get caught. But I will decide when. Jonny, think about it. Me in the witness box, spilling all. Okay, my killing lacked subtlety, but I was never arrogant. Seriously, I ask the two of you, do you think the British Government wants me in a witness box? I don't think so. Like you, Jon, I'm sort of risk-bipolar. I'm liable to say and do anything. Anyway, can you imagine what I'm going to do to the Pontiff? Can you imagine the state he will be in? No, I will take my time. I have been planning this return for years. He'll be squealing for his mammy, too. I found that bizarre. Grown men crying for their mammy when getting what they deserve. Creepy, really. I didn't expect that. Men in their sixties crying for their mammy. Saturn finally settled over dear old Derry, eh, Jon? And there's me, seeing everything. I have been watching you all. Do you know how easy it is to put on a white forensic suit with a mask and walk into a PSNI crime scene? In this day and age? You fools. Abigail Burns, eh, Jon? Did you tell Anna there what you'd like to do to Abigail? Go on. I know you've thought about it. Just waiting, eh? Same old Jon. Waiting to make your move.'

'You've flipped, Gerry. Not without cause, but why murder innocents?'

Anna listened, afraid to move. It was as if Valberg and O'Driscoll knew each other.

'Don't fuck with me, Jon. Innocent? My father was innocent. *I* was innocent.'

Anna said, 'For God's sake, it's got to stop. It has to stop.'

Anna now understood Valberg's analysis of the situation, even from her brief time in the presence of what she believed to be a psychotic. She began to think the Pope was right, that she should not have come. But Anna was where she was as a result of her own decision. She could do nothing but adapt and survive. All thought would have to be nullified. Survival would be all that mattered. The last time she had felt this sense of numbness was when she discovered her husband was having an affair. That unfortunate episode and all the gossip surrounding it were the worst things that had happened to her. But they paled now, meaningless when weighed against matters of life and death, against kneeling beside a van bomb with a gun trained on her head by a madman with a grudge. O'Driscoll was in charge now. Whatever he said had to be done. Just do it. Comply or die.

'Anna. Can I call you Anna?' O'Driscoll asked.

'Yes.'

'I wanted to make sure you heard all this in the right conditions. Well, my conditions. Everything you need on the Pope is contained on the memory cards of the two mobile phones that will detonate the bombs in the van here and on Craigavon Bridge. There is no bomb on the Peace Bridge, but a little present for Jon. I need plenty of diversions. You understand. If the bombs detonate, you will have nothing. Well, you and a lot of others will die. But if you get the evidence, guess what? I will allow due process of law. Ain't that just dandy? You see, Jon thinks I've flipped, but there you go. A little test for you. Now, the vermin is well protected, but if you have evidence and due process, I'll watch it all and see that fucker squirm, and I just might leave him be. But if you don't get the evidence, well, a lot of people will die. Now, the PSNI don't want that again. Not yet. Another failure to protect life. Not another bunch of entries for a new edition of *Lost Lives*. Naw. Definitely not. Not another load of victims. At worst, you will expose Mr Pontiff for what he is, and that's what I want. I want it done publicly. Now, just on that, do we have an agreement?'

Anna, with more confidence now. 'If we have proper evidence we can use, of course we will deal with it.'

'I won't get involved in semantics but I will take that as an agreement.'

Valberg asked, 'Well, what if we don't get the evidence?'

'Jon, I visited your father, you know. I wanted to thank him, but I couldn't speak to him. I stood in his room ... '

'No way.'

'You didn't know. Just before he died. You were asleep in the next room. I stood there. I let him see me. Took off my disguise. It's amazing what you get away with wearing black-rimmed glasses. *Fist of Fury*. Bruce Lee. On another note, I've watched *Enter the Dragon* ninety-six times. Going for the hundred. Brilliant disguise in *Fist of Fury*, though. The Chinese telephone guy. Sort of goofy. *Fist of Fury*. That's my all-time favourite. Anyway, the goofy-telephone-guy disguise was just brilliant. Those glasses. I use them all the time. Different ones.'

'What are you talking about?'

'Well, Jon, your dad put out his hand to me. Ah, enough of that. Well, you know Bruce Lee had many disguises in *Fist of Fury* and hung all those bodies up publicly. In revenge. I spent a life killing. It's all I know. But it's over now. Just the Pope left. And Councillor McFlynn, he's alive. I let him go. Another great agent of the not so great British state. His fate will come to pass soon, too. He's not long for this world. He's the victim of an attempted murder, too. You made sure of that by sneaking him away. Naughty boy, Jonny. You entrapped the pontificator and his wide boys well, there. Well done. But sure then all your suspicions were confirmed.'

'What suspicions? What do you know? Tell us.'

'Funny how it all comes together. My father. His cause of

death: "crushed and disfigured". Blockage of the respiratory tract as a result of the heavy accumulation of debris due to an explosion. Can you think of the images of the type of death he had when you read something like that in a pathologist's report? As a child, that is. As a boy. Can you think how hot that would make your blood boil? My blood has been boiling for years. Trained by the British Army to kill. To kill. To do nothing but kill. Everywhere and anyone. I made enough money privately after the dirty war here. You think it's over? No way. With so many unresolved killings? Appalling.'

'Well, how many did you kill?' asked Valberg.

'Too many, Jon, my friend. But, Jon, do you know what it's like having your father blown up and your mother slit her wrists and die?'

'No. I don't.'

'Those early days in prison, in solitary confinement for my own protection, that taught me a lot about the depths of human nature and depravity. Add that to the way my mother and father died. I tried the faith thing. I tried to believe everything I was taught at school. I did try. Just like you, amigo, searching for your faith. Your god.'

'It does not justify murder. Never. It's even a spurious plea in mitigation.'

'Well, listen to you as the blood stops flowing to your hands and arms and puts you at a disadvantage when you try and defuse the van bomb here. Listen to you. Well, if you survive this, you find out who does the Pope's laundry now. You check it all. Dickey and Montgomery. Just two grunting pigs. Properly in hell now. Truth? That's a joke. That thing at the bottom of a bottomless black well. Down there with the rats, Jon.'

'Gentlemen,' said Anna, 'this is all very interesting, but what about the bombs? Please.'

'Okay, Anna. Don't get hysterical, now. Quickly, then, before they try to shoot me. The bombs are on a timer and an overriding phone detonator. Nothing complicated. Very new. Very easy. You just remove the BlackBerry phones, disconnect, and all stops. You have all you need, then. If you are too late, the bombs explode, you die, and no evidence.

No, don't move yet or I will shoot you. I recorded all my calls with our dear friend. His involvement with the Force Research Unit and the Cromwell Killers is all there. And guess what, I even set up a website about him which, if you follow the instructions on the phones, you can activate. Then, Jon, no doubt Miss Cleary in the *Derry Journal* will print all that stuff you gave her from your father. I don't know what it is, but I suspect … Well, I'll leave that. By the way, those marksmen have orders to shoot you both as well, if necessary. Good friends, eh? What are they for? Now, up and run, Anna. You have fifteen minutes to get to Craigavon Bridge. Back of the lorry, sitting on a little docking station on top of the bomb. Just unplug it. If either of you fails, hell will be unleashed. And one last thing – only you two can detach the phones. I have encoded your prints and they will only respond to your touch. Trust me, I'm not bluffing. Go now, Anna. Jon, you stay. Neither of you look back.'

Anna got up, steadied herself, and ran as fast as she could. She wanted to turn around. She wanted to be sure Valberg would do what he had been told but she raced on.

As Anna ran towards her colleagues, some of them thought she was trying to escape. Shouts of 'Cover her! Cover her!' split the night silence and a volley of shots rang out. O'Driscoll's warning flashed again in Anna's head and she threw herself to the ground. Linda jumped into the nearest police car and sped to her. Everyone was shouting now at the same time. Confusion reigned. More rounds crashed over Anna's head in the general direction of the van behind her. Linda screeched to a halt beside Anna who scrambled up and dived into the back seat. She shouted to Linda to get to Craigavon Bridge at top speed.

On Foyle Bridge, Valberg was flat on the ground. O'Driscoll ran out from cover, grabbed him, and pulled him to safety at the back of the van. There was a lull in the shooting. O'Driscoll switched off the van lights and stood calmly at the back of the vehicle. He was wearing PSNI fatigues with protective armour and a balaclava mask, all in black. Valberg realised it must be part of his escape plan.

'Jon, please forgive me. No-one believed in me except your father.'

'And your mother. She did, too. And at least Father Doherty.'

O'Driscoll was backing away from the van to the railings.

'Gerry, don't!' Valberg put his hand out.

Valberg saw only O'Driscoll's eyes. O'Driscoll raised himself with his back to the high bridge railings. He turned to jump over and a single shot echoed in the dark. Valberg heard a groan and O'Driscoll was gone. He fell into the darkness. Valberg dared not move from the back of the van as more bullets peppered the air around him.

Before long, silence descended again on Foyle Bridge

With the van's rear doors open Valberg looked at what O'Driscoll had described. He saw the BlackBerry on a small docking station and detached it. A timer started, and Valberg was sure it was a trap. Going over the side of bridge was not an option for him. Neither was staying. There was no choice but to run for it.

Valberg raced towards Culmore, the mobile safely in his hands, shouting as loudly as he could to take cover. Everyone took heed apart from Michael who – just as Linda had done moments before – commandeered a police car he was standing beside and drove straight to Valberg. As soon as Michael set off the van bomb exploded.

The explosion threw Valberg to the ground and Michael almost ran over him but stopped just in time. Michael jumped out and helped Valberg to his feet.

'That fucking Brit was right. Duck and cover. Jesus,' Valberg panted, breathless from his sprint.

It wasn't a chemical or 'dirty' device, just enough conventional explosives to destroy the van with white phosphorous burning in a rage inside of what was left.

There was no chance of any forensic possibilities. Fire crews, followed by police and ambulance, rushed towards the scene. Valberg was fine and O'Driscoll gone. Dead from a bullet before he hit the water, Valberg thought, or dead on impact. No-one could survive such a drop in Valberg's opinion.

Valberg took the wheel and they sped with a police escort, sirens screaming, towards the city centre.

CHAPTER 33

Anna Harte had to assume command at Craigavon Bridge. She explained the situation quickly in just enough time for the British Army bomb-disposal team to get some protection on her. Two of the team drove Anna, all suited up and with full headgear, to the back of the lorry. She had no gloves on so that the phone would react to her touch if that were necessary. There was no time to gamble to see if O'Driscoll was bluffing. She told the army team to leave her, but they refused in case she needed some assistance.

Anna was convinced she was going to die now. The magnitude of what she was about to do, what had happened and what could happen, almost overwhelmed her. Her mind drifted, as Valberg's did at times, for self-preservation or the appearance of being professional and calm under intense pressure. For a moment she wished herself back at school with her older sister and her mother consoling her, hugging her and kissing her. That was all a world and a lifetime away. All gone now forever.

She looked down towards the Foyle Bridge and saw fire lighting up the Derry skyline. Was Jon still alive? She had no way of knowing. What a night. She had to be strong now and prayed that O'Driscoll hadn't lied to her.

With a small torch gripped between her teeth to light the device, Anna removed the second BlackBerry from the docking station in the back of the lorry. The army personnel looked on nervously. As she lifted the phone, she smelled burning of some sort and heard hissing. The lorry was packed with incendiary material about to erupt. She shook off what she could of the protective gear, jumped back into the military vehicle with the phone and sped back to safety. Behind her, a deafening explosion blew the lorry apart and flames lit up the night sky.

In the noise and confusion, Anna did not notice Valberg and Michael emerge through the police cordon. They had seen everything. Valberg called Anna and they fell into each other's arms.

'God, Jon, I thought we were never going to make it,' Anna cried.

'It's over. You're alive. That's all that matters. You have people to face. Get it together. Here, take this.' He handed her the other BlackBerry. 'I don't want it. I want to go to sleep. That's all I want. Sleep and a drink. You have to face the public now. You're the new Chief of police. You do it. I have to get out of here.'

'What happened to O'Driscoll? Did they get him?'

'He's gone.'

'Gone as in dead?'

'Shot, I think. And then he went over the bridge.'

'He must be dead, then. No-one could survive that.'

'Must be. But ... who knows?'

Anna was on the verge of crying as Valberg hugged her again, well out of sight of the media. He then pulled his jacket tightly around him and turned away into the night. Anna realised what she had to do now.

Amid the screaming fire engines and lights going back on over Derry and the search for O'Driscoll's body beginning, pictures were broadcast all around the world as the media got closer to the action. The PSNI rushed out their own carefully edited footage and made several official statements aimed at calming the hysteria across the city. It was important for the police to get their version of events in the public domain quickly.

CHAPTER 34

Valberg, shattered and bruised, walked down John Street towards the Foyle embankment. He went straight to the river and watched all that was going on. He thought of Janice Sloan, the young girl he had made the mistake of having compassion for all those years before. He stood opposite where he'd found her drunk and confused and trying to help a badly injured man. If he could just do that stupid thing we all wish we could do, he thought: turn back time. He would have lifted the knife he was so pleased to find and thrown it in the river. There would be no evidence. No charge. No remand and no suicide. If he could just change that one thing. What a difference that would make.

As he walked towards the Peace Bridge, he listened to the sounds of chaos and sirens everywhere. What a week. Police along the embankment recognised him and he was allowed a clear passage. Chief Superintendent David Kells, his long-suffering boss at Strand Road Station who had been called back from his annual leave because of the bomb threats, met him at the bridge.

'Here, this is for you, Jon. It was taped to the railings of the bridge. The army tech guys checked it so it's okay. Your name is typed on it. Evidence or what? You decide. It's your case. It's bagged up but not recorded.'

He handed Valberg a small package.

'Thanks, David.'

'Will you sleep now, Jon? Jesus, you need it. You're in an awful state.'

'Maybe later, David. It's a bloody mess ... What sort of

police service will we have this time tomorrow, eh? He's well gone now and for the best, I think. I really don't care what happens to him.'

'The Pope or O'Driscoll, Jon?'

'Good one, David. Nice. See you later. We are the walking fuckin' dead.'

Valberg continued along the embankment towards Strand Road. Before starting up Lower Clarendon Street, he stopped again and looked at the package. He was going to throw it in the river unopened. He had had enough. The Foyle and Craigavon bridges were still smouldering. Not really knowing why, he tore away the clear forensics bag and opened the tightly wrapped package. Inside was an aged copy of *Death of a Naturalist* and a note.

Jon,

It's a first edition. I was keeping it for your father, I always hoped he would make it. But you may have it now. Don't worry, I got it legitimately. Sorry for all the diversions, but I had to tie everyone up to give me the best chance to get away. It was all part of the Nemesis Project. It took a lot of planning. Years, in fact. I was pretty sure you would make it to read this. I can only hope I do as well. In case I didn't get to say how grateful I was for your father's belief in me, I do that now. He kept me alive and in some way allowed me to get my revenge. People in this cruel life seldom get that chance, or redemption. Or, of course, that golden oldie, salvation. I have had a lifetime of killing, cover-up and distortion. There are others like me, too, but many never come back here. Take care, Jon. I'm almost finished and if I make it through tonight I will keep a close eye on the pious Pontiff from afar, and closer by if needs be. You know I am a murderer now. So be it. Do what you have to do, Jon, and so will I.

I'll be in touch.

The note was not signed.

Valberg wanted to throw everything into the river but couldn't. The book was supposed to be a present for his father so he had to keep it. The evidential value meant nothing to Valberg now and, strangely, he found some honesty in O'Driscoll's words. He rambled and fell into insanity, but Valberg found him credible … to a point.

Valberg put the book and the note in his inside jacket pocket. O'Driscoll was deranged, for certain, but now his killing and the nature of it made some sense, although despicable and cowardly to any reasonable human being. It was also clear to Valberg that the killings were easy for O'Driscoll and they inflicted unadulterated fear and terror in the minds of the Derry public. Thirty years of conflict in the North of Ireland had not scared the people of Derry as much as O'Driscoll's maniacal killing spree.

Valberg had intended to go to the operations room at Strand Road but realised it would be hectic there. He needed to rest. Some time alone. Time to think. He headed home.

CHAPTER 35

With the immediate danger over, residents returned to their homes the next day and the city got back to normal. The *Derry Journal* produced a special edition with the headline 'Diary of a Naturalist'. This was the publication of Gustav Valberg's court notes from O'Driscoll's trial with his innermost thoughts and analysis revealed. Amanda Cleary had compiled the edition and had included damning details of the roles Dickey, Montgomery and their boss, the Chief Constable of the PSNI, had played. The revelations were shocking. For the first time, the public were made aware that everyone on the original jury, apart from Gustav, had convicted O'Driscoll for irrational or sectarian reasons. It was clear Gerard O'Driscoll was innocent.

The Pope's nightmare was only beginning. The Historical Enquiries Team did not need much impetus to start an investigative review. The Pope had to resign. Worse, he faced potential charges of murder, attempted murder and perverting the course of justice. He needed to be in a secure location now, for sure.

Swanky Frankie was found alive but so addled with alcohol that he could recall nothing. Sidney Rankin was reported missing. A search was underway, but not as intense as the one for O'Driscoll's body in the River Foyle.

With O'Driscoll's name in the public domain now and with the publication of Gustav Valberg's notes, Orla Harkin's family understandably wanted the investigation into Orla's death opened again. That was another job for the Historical Enquiries Team and, potentially, the Police Ombudsman's Office.

When Orla's elderly mother presented herself at Strand Road Police Station shortly after she read the *Derry Journal* articles, she only wanted to talk to Valberg. Ignoring the burglars, thieves and drug dealers reporting for bail at the public desk, Dottie Harkin pushed her way in with the aid of a walking stick and presented herself for justice, thinking Valberg could deliver.

'He's the only one who can find out what happened to my Orla. Harte's a bigwig now and probably on her way back to Belfast. Orla's daddy died of a broken heart. You tell Mr Valberg I won't rest until I get the truth and justice. Where's Mr Valberg? Tell him to call and see me. I'm begging. Just begging. I thought we got justice years ago for Orla but it turns out not so here I am. Who's gonnie take up Orla's case now? Who? You police are all the same. You think I'm some sort of disease. Not clean enough for justice. You'd all like us to go away and move on, eh? My wee girl. I sent her to her death. My Orla. She was all we had. She was everything. Aye, Orla's case. Who'll march up and down the Strand Road for me and Orla, demanding justice? No-one, I tell you. No-one. PSNI, RUC, B-Specials. You're all the same. I just want justice. I just want … I just want to remember how Orla lived. Not how she died. Now I can't. It's all starting again. Now I'm to be treated like that wee boy's mother. We were all wrong. All of us. We're all gonnie burn in hell.'

The harassed sergeant who was called to speak to Mrs Harkin at reception could only inform her that DCI Valberg was not on duty and that she would be better making an appointment to see him.

Mrs Harkin broke down crying. Her grief was personal but public. The death had destroyed her life and her husband's. She had already forgiven the young man who did not kill Orla in a letter to O'Driscoll's mother, providing perhaps a modicum of consolation for the tormented woman before she took her own life. Now Mrs Harkin was begging for truth and justice in her old age, grief stricken and alone. She felt guilty about everything and ashamed. She felt guilty about sending her daughter out for a pint of milk nearly thirty years ago. She felt guilty that O'Driscoll was wrongfully charged with killing Orla and convicted for it. And she felt guilty and ashamed for once believing in the due process of law. She had believed all that the police had told her. Her faith in the justice system was shattered.

Dottie Harkin left the police station in tears, inconsolable with guilt, anger and sadness. She hobbled out onto the Strand Road and stood silently on the pavement. In the distance, a large passenger bus gathered speed as it passed through traffic lights at a nearby junction. In her confused and distressed state, a terrible thought flashed through her head: it was time to end it all. All the pain and the suffering. She saw the bus driver talk and joke with a passenger. Dottie was about to step into oblivion when a firm hand on her shoulder gently restrained her and she heard someone speak.

'Careful there, dear.'

Dottie looked around to see a tall stranger wearing glasses smiling at her. She was suddenly grateful he had brought her to her senses.

'Thank you, son. God bless you and protect you and your family.'

'It's quite alright,' the polite reply came. Then he walked on.

Dottie limped slowly back to the Lecky Road, where she lived on her own. She went into Orla's room, knelt down slowly by her daughter's bed and began a decade of the rosary.

CHAPTER 36

A new fear settled over Derry the longer Sidney Rankin was missing and Gerard O'Driscoll's body could not be found. O'Driscoll was becoming even more legendary, and his previous employers in London were growing fearful, too. This was their worst nightmare. Other supposed agents of the British Government dared to raise their heads in the media, claiming to know O'Driscoll. But they were the usual mix of fantasists and drug-addicted failures who had nothing to offer but more misery and lies. The British Government turned its back on all of them. No-one in the city trusted or believed them. What the public did believe was that O'Driscoll was a cold-blooded and ruthless killer now but he was not responsible for the death of Orla Harkin in 1982.

Detective Constable Finbar Callaghan's funeral had been delayed by all the murder and mayhem. Eventually, it was held at St Eugene's Cathedral amid huge security. Thousands turned out to pay their respects, among them Acting Chief Constable Anna Harte.

Valberg did not want to go to the funeral service, not out of disrespect but from his own guilt and fear. He felt guilty it was not he who had been killed, and he was terrified of meeting Finbar's parents. He tortured himself over whether to go, but with his mother and Anna by his side, he made it. His left hand did shake once during the service, but only Valberg's mother noticed. She placed her own hand on her son's to steady it.

Valberg planned to get totally drunk after the funeral. He had a bottle of his special red Brunello wine in mind that he intended to drink on his own, and whatever else he could get. The thought of the wine kept him focused. He could taste and smell it throughout the solemn service presided over by the weakening Father James Doherty.

Valberg was close to breaking point. It had been such a punishing time, made all the more brutal by what Finbar's mother told him when they met. 'He really looked up to you,' she said. 'You were a great friend to him. Finbar just wanted to be the policeman you are, the person you are. He admired you so much. If you don't mind me saying, Mr Valberg, Finbar thought and talked of you at home a bit like the big brother he never had. Thank you for all your kindness towards him. Thank you.'

'I'm really sorry. It should have been me.'

'No. It is the Lord's way. I just wanted to thank you for being so good to him. You are a good man, Mr Valberg. I have heard all about you. We will bury our beautiful son now.'

Valberg felt so awkward. He knew he was far from good. He felt a failure all his life as a big brother. That well-intentioned comment made it certain he would drink a lot of alcohol soon. The tears began to build.

As Finbar's coffin was readied to leave the church amid the smell of burning incense, a young girl sang *Let It Be*. The song broke Valberg, but his mother steadied him again. He had to help carry the coffin to the funeral car so he quickly composed himself. He made it to the front of the mourners, still displaying signs of emotion and grief he had not exhibited even at his father's funeral or in any such public way before.

What Valberg really wanted was the wine.

He just had to get to that Brunello waiting for him. He had brought back many bottles from Tuscany and imported more. He kept them for moments of deep depression, like the one he could sense enveloping him now. The Brunello's effect would be dangerously hallucinogenic, but the taste was worth it. He was content to pay the wine's high price but never counted the emotional cost to himself or those who tried to get close to him.

Valberg could not face going to the cemetery. He had a room booked in the City Hotel. He was going there to lock himself in alone.

As Valberg stood in the grounds of St Eugene's Cathedral watching Finbar's cortege preparing to leave, Anna Harte called him to one side. They stood in a secluded spot close to the towering edifice. Her greatly increased security detail watched from a distance, on edge due to the proximity of the church to the Bogside.

'Jesus, Anna, you can't move anywhere now on your own,' Valberg said, glancing at the retinue of plain-clothes policemen. 'Here. Take these.'

'Take what?'

'My ID and weapon. I'm finished. Done. I don't want it all anymore.'

Anna had to move in closer to him.

'Don't you dare, Jon Valberg. Don't you dare.'

'And don't tell me the service needs people like me. Don't say that.'

'For God's sake, Jon, don't be the predictable, disillusioned everyman. I have enough of those around me. Please.'

'No. Take them, Anna.'

'What is it that you want? Your own forensic team in Derry with their own building and facilities? No more of this Belfast nonsense? Is that what you want? Are we negotiating here or what? Negotiating over and about the dead? What do you want? For Christ's sake. Jesus.'

'Take them and go, Anna. You're making those guys nervous. And tell the others.'

'Tell them what, Jon? We need you.'

'No you don't. You think you do. If you find O'Driscoll, your problems are only starting. He'll find you and the Pope when it suits him. I don't know how, but he got away. What he did here was chicken feed to him. I'm tired. I'm sick of it all. No more, Anna. I've had enough this time.'

'You know Carlin will be charged soon. I've thought about a lot of things, especially just now at the funeral. I agree with the Director of the PPS that it would be best to wait, but he will have to be charged.'

'I won't ask where he is.'

'Don't.'

'Anna, take these and let me go.'

'You leave me little choice. I'll take them. But for your protection only. Six weeks unofficially. Three weeks officially. Contact me anytime. As far as everyone is concerned, you're on holiday for three weeks. See how you feel then, and if you still don't want to come back, take another three weeks. I'll keep these safe. Now I am going. I have work to do.'

'Goodbye, Anna,' Valberg said and watched as her security team hustled her away.

CHAPTER 37

Valberg followed Finbar's funeral procession a while as it made its way along the Lone Moor Road to the city cemetery. He then turned left down Westland Street and walked through the Bogside en route to the City Hotel. As usual, he ignored every direction from his superiors and advice about his own personal safety. If a malcontent dissident republican still trying to free Ireland had him in his sights, so be it, he thought.

He was conscious he was near to Cable Street, where Majella McLaughlin had been murdered. There had been enough killing here over so many years. It had to stop. Life was moving on. The tourists who had booked their trips to the city were brave enough to come, and they were being guided around the Bogside like herds of nervous sheep. Most stood at Free Derry Corner for group and single photographs. Valberg could tell they were amazed by the murals and wondered if they understood their significance.

Valberg did not envy the tour guides, especially now. After the number and manner of the recent murders, so well reported, most of the discussions must have been laced with gloom and doom. He always found it strange to see tourists wandering the streets of the Bogside. Now they would be up on the Derry Walls as well, and perhaps the recent killings would form part of their trip. Valberg was certain it was not part of O'Driscoll's plan to boost the tourist industry in Derry.

Finally, as one group of Italian tourists moved away from the Bloody Sunday Memorial and before another arrived,

Valberg picked his moment to stop and contemplate on the city's most tragic time in living memory. He stared intently at the names that had been burned into his consciousness from when he first came to Derry. He remembered telling Finbar about the hurricane of bullets that swept through the Bogside, devastating innocent lives and families, leaving behind heartbreak and anguish.

Valberg stood there, remembering all he could about Finbar and how his thoughtful act that fateful day had changed both their worlds forever. Then he stepped away to allow another group of tourists to pay their respects at the memorial.

Suddenly a dark wave of sadness and depression came over Valberg. He knew he had to go. It was time to confront his demons.

CHAPTER 38

Valberg had booked in to the City Hotel earlier and left all the alcohol he thought he would need and spare clothes in his room overlooking the river. He locked the door and hung the 'Do Not Disturb' sign outside. For extra security he jammed a chair against the door handle. He made it clear to the hotel staff he did not want disturbed. Peace at last, on his own, and a chance to drink and sleep and reflect on so many things that had happened in such a short time. He was suffering from information overload and needed time to decompress.

As he began to drink his beloved Brunello straight from the bottle, he dispassionately observed the work going on below to get the Peace Bridge finished for launch day. After a few hours, the alcohol kicked in and his mind began to drift from reality.

He saw himself standing in a circle with the Pope and O'Driscoll, guns pointed at each other's heads, wondering who would be the first to shoot or want to be shot. Valberg felt like a coward. He was hiding from his difficulties, personal and professional, in that contemptible way – with the aid of alcohol. He was consumed with guilt and shame for Finbar's death. Valberg wished it had been him who was blown up. He deserved to die. Justice demanded it. He believed he should have saved many of the innocent people recently slaughtered and that really he was no better than O'Driscoll. Just as bad, maybe.

After he finished the second bottle of Brunello, exhaustion set in. He remembered he had brought a copy of *Death of a*

Naturalist with him. The first edition O'Driscoll had gotten for his father. He pulled it out of his jacket and sat on the floor, his back to the bed, drinking from a large bottle of vodka mixed with orange juice. He was getting comfortably numb now.

Valberg did his best to read some random verses out loud but he struggled to get Seamus Heaney's voice right. He read incoherently. It lacked all dignity. He repeated 'dark drop' and 'trapped sky' over and over and tried to make it sound as meaningful and poetic as it was written but failed miserably. He was laboured and slow amid heavy breathing and attempts to cry. The vodka bottle was empty.

Valberg slipped into a dead, alcohol-filled sleep and only roused several hours later. He immediately reached for another bottle of vodka and began to drink again.

Soon, the ghosts were back.

He saw the Sultan swinging and crying for his mammy. He saw him being sliced open. He heard the squelch of the blood slowly pumping out of Paddy Sharkey's neck. Valberg kicked his heels against the hotel-room floor, imitating Paddy's last act of defiance, thinking about him being decapitated. He saw himself in Majella McLaughlin's house, pinned to the sofa, unable to move. A young girl came in and stared at Valberg. A call from the kitchen was telling her to hurry up and go for the milk before her Daddy came home from work for his tea.

'Don't go. It's not safe out there,' Valberg pleaded to the imaginary child.

He could not stop her leaving. He started sobbing and cursing. He was convinced Majella McLaughlin was hanging upside down in his hotel room watching him. Images came to him faster now but in muddled form. Majella swung to and fro. His friend Gerry stood in front of him and took off his thick-rimmed black glasses.

'Hello, Jon. What are you doing down there? Searching for the devil? He's everywhere. Would you like to lead an army against the devil? Now, ain't that just dandy. La-di-dah. Here we are, a right pair of misfit murderers, eh? I cut, you hold. A great team, eh? I kill, you watch. I escape, you help. I laugh, you cry. I slice, you hold, and I smell the blood of an Apprentice Boy. I kill, you live. You had me kill all those poor bastards who made your daddy sick, and I got my revenge. You know, Jon, it's the two-lives thing. My life before Orla Harkin and my life after Orla Harkin. Or my life before my father was murdered and my life after. Same for you. Your life before little Patrick died and your life after. We all have a split somewhere. A moment that defines us. Determines our future. Any more wee disgusting dirty little jobs, evil Jonny? I don't need to get paid anymore. I kill for free. How about a wee rumble somewhere? A real bomb. Eh, Jon? Let's get the old team back together again. Or better still, here's a few good lines for you from the Policeman's Prayer, as God knows you need it now:

'Give us cool heads, stout hearts, hard punches, an uncanny flair for investigation, and wise judgement. Make us the terror of burglars, the friend of children and law-abiding citizens, kind to strangers, polite to bores, strict with law-breakers, and impervious to temptations. Saint Michael, your hard knocks that so surprised the devil, and your angelic self-control give us inspiration.

'God, if only that were you, eh, Jon? If you could guard a great city of men, women and children. But here you are. Joint-enterprise, man. My co-conspirator. Jonny, you naughty boy. Now I'm not in a negative place, so I have a bit of feeling. I mean, I'm in a good state of mind. Not a killing one just now. I'm not split off from reality tonight, Jon, like you there. Just this once. For you, Jonny, I'll stop the killing for a while.'

'Fuck you. Get away. Leave me alone. Bastard. Go away.'

'Look at you. My goodness, you are a disgrace. Come on, just one more cut. One more sip. Some more dangerous stuff before you say kiss, kiss, bye-bye to that Carolina one. Adios, amigo. Kiss, kiss, bye-bye to little Maria, too. Our little devils come in many forms. Devils in battalions. Another dirty little secret. Here I am now. Your devil, Jon. Fee-fi-fo-fum. I smell the blood of an Orangeman. Or did you see Finbar's blood? Naw, none of it. Burnt and deformed. Another closed coffin and another. And it goes on and on and on forever. Closed coffins in perpetuity. Oh, here he is. Hello, Finbar. He's on the floor there. Drunk as a skunk. Out of it.

Air-locked and void of reason. I'm sure he'll be glad to see you.'

'Finbar. Is that you? I'm sorry. So fucking sorry.'

'Oh, aye, sir. It's me. Here, I have something for you. Take these keys. I've stocked it with all the usual music. King Crimson, Metallica, Tool and Rush. All there in your lovely Saab 900. Got you an old one all cleaned up and as good as new. Only a million miles on it but going great anyway. Just put the key in, turn that ignition on, and off you go on your superhighway. Here, I'll go get it for you. Here, watch me blow myself up again. That was good, wasn't it? Not much time for my life to flash before me. Just a quick millisecond before death. Then I am torn apart and the rest of me melts and burns. Sort of like a bump on the head, really. That whoosh of the implosion. Ever hear about that from any bomb survivors, sir? Whoosh, then bang. Aye, and it's true. You don't hear the bang at all. Just a wee thump and a knock on your head, or in my case my head exploding and leaving my body. It didn't even blow off. It blew up and vanished. I think me poor ma and da buried a coffin of sand. The undertaker lied and so did Father Doherty. Not just about identifying my remains but something else. Did he ever tell you who really killed Orla? Maybe you should ask and tell Psycho Balls here, the malignant narcissist. He's gone now. Aye, a coffin of sand. That's what you all put in the ground. God, don't exhume me whatever you do, and keep my parents away from any trial or inquest. Do you think they got my weight right when they filled my closed casket with sand? I was trying to shed a few pounds. Thanks to you I achieved that anyway. Ask Father Doherty what really happened to Orla Harkin. I dare you.'

Valberg was paralysed with fear now and shaking violently. He could not speak to Finbar. The words would not come out. He was dipping in and out of consciousness. He had slipped onto his back and tried to sit up straight and drink more vodka to stop the hallucinations. He looked around the room to see who was there. The only constants were Billy Black and Majella McLaughlin swinging above him. Trying to sit up and drink more made him worse. He was spilling vodka all over himself. He felt listless and weak.

Valberg dragged himself to his feet. As he rose unsteadily, he caught a reflection in the mirror. Was it Valberg or O'Driscoll? He could not tell in his befuddled state. It looked like O'Driscoll in black military fatigues and balaclava mask. This figure ready for battle was Valberg's reflection. He had to remove the mask. This was the real killer, the real murderer all this time. This was the revelation he had been waiting on. This would be his true confession and fate. Who was the killer behind the mask? Who was this living killing machine? Majella and Billy already knew – they had suffered grievously at his hands.

Valberg stumbled and thought he could see Michael with his notebook out along with Anna and Linda reflected in the mirror, too.

'Well, ma'am, like I said, it doesn't make sense. You didn't actually see anyone else on the Foyle Bridge. I've checked my notes. I can't find Detective Valberg leaving the hospital. He's lost on the CCTV footage, and all that emerges is a figure dressed as a cleaner with long hair, a beard and thick glasses. He kills Detectives Dickey and Montgomery. Detective Valberg knew they were coming. He told me. The size, build and height are all very similar. Someone had access to our systems. Maybe there are two people really, ma'am, or they are acting together. Then you take Billy Black. Detective Valberg had me convinced on the first day it was a one-man job. Maybe it is or it was. I dunno. It's all in my notes. Well, one more thing, ma'am. Finbar and the cart before the horse. Aye, Valberg put the cart before the horse. He looked and then the bang. His body was almost moving before the bang. It wasn't bang and roar and run. It was look over, flinch, and then the bang and run, and hysterics. Aye, ma'am. Cart before the horse for sure.'

Linda just laughed. Then Anna started laughing. And Michael joined in. All now on Valberg's hotel bed. All the while Majella and Billy were swinging. Majella was praying, holding her rosary beads, saying over and over: 'Our Father, deliver us from evil.' Billy Black was crying: 'Mammy, Mammy.'

Valberg turned to the killer in the mirror. He took off the mask in terror, revealing himself as the Saturn Killer. He

shouted 'No!' and tried to kick the mirror but only succeed-
ed in falling to the floor again. Inconsolable, guilty, desperate. Valberg was finished. His life was over. He was going to
burn alone in hell forever.

Valberg did not know how long he lay there. Dreams and
hallucinations blended, merged, disappeared.

Then Valberg heard someone calling his name.

'Who is it? Who's there?' Valberg thought it was someone
at the door.

But it was Patrick, calling his big brother.

'No, Patrick. No. Go away. Don't call me. So sorry. Please
excuse me. I never meant to hurt anyone. Never meant to
hurt anyone.'

'Jon. Jon. Jon! Come on. This way, Jon. Daddy's waiting.
Jon, here. Take my hand. Hold my hand, Jon, just until
Daddy comes. Don't let my hand go. Don't.'

But Valberg's grip on his brother's tiny hand was slipping.
Then Patrick was quiet. He lay on the ground. Motionless.
Silent. Valberg's father asked what had happened.

'Jon, what have you done? I told you to wait there. I told
you to hold his hand and not let go. I told you. Patrick.
Breathe. Patrick. Patrick. Oh, no. Patrick!'

Valberg believed it was he, as a child, who had killed his
little brother. The great family secret. The one thing that
must never be mentioned. It became such a secret of secrets
that a lie became the truth. Valberg's parents convinced
themselves of a different version of events, and so it became
their gospel truth. This truth that protected their son so he
did not grow up knowing he had been told to hold his brother's hand and had let that innocent hand slip, letting his
little brother run into the bumper of an oncoming black se-
dan. All that was done was for the best, and Valberg's father
took the blame for something he had not done right to the
end as he lay riddled with cancer, in agony, with no legs.
He took the responsibility of protecting his living son so seriously that he convinced himself he was the one who had
let little Patrick's hand go. It was all suppressed and swept
under the carpet, like dirt. It was a dirty secret Valberg was
finding out about now as he hit rock bottom. If the real truth
came out he would have to kill himself. He could never live

with the guilt and shame. He felt humiliated and sick.

He was in the witness box in front of a jury. His worst nightmare. All those solicitors and barristers he had been so critical of were standing up one by one, asking him deeply personal questions.

'Tell the truth, Mr Valberg. What have you to fear from the truth? The truth pure and simple. Not as you or your dead father would like it to be. But the truth pure and simple. Pure and simple.'

Then they would all laugh at him.

'You are not a perjurious individual, Mr Valberg, are you? You took an oath. So help you God. You must believe in God. You do, don't you? Or was that a lie, too? Did you lie when you took the oath, Mr Valberg? Please tell us the truth.'

The witness box was a furnace.

It was hot again. Valberg was sweating. He watched little Patrick put his hand in a blazing fire, but his brother felt no pain as his flesh melted and his hand was reduced to a bright pink stump and the white heat incinerated everything.

Valberg looked for water to pour on the fire, but Patrick was not in pain. He smiled at his big brother and waved goodbye.

'Patrick. My friend, my brother. I loved you so much. If there was one thing I wish I could change. That would make such a difference. Patrick, I'm so sorry. Let me be your brother again. Let me protect you. I love you, Patrick. I will do better the next time. Give me a chance. I'm so sorry.'

Valberg looked everywhere for water. He needed it. He wanted to hear and see the movement of a river. He fought hard for that sound, that image. Then he found it. The sounds of nature in spring that he had loved so much when fishing with his father. At last, some peace. Running water and the sound of the whip and whiz of a fly rod as the line sliced the surface. His father's encouraging words comforted him.

'Formless, Jon. Like water. Become the water. The river. Adapt. Relax that arm. It's all in the wrist. How does that feel, Jon? I love the sound of the reel when you pull the line out. Beautiful. Remember, grasp the line gently in one hand and let the fly float and your line out. Keep a good eye on the fly. That's it, Jon, well done.'

This was all Valberg wanted. Alone with his father again as his father cast out his line with laser precision, a Cut Throat Cat fly on the end. The only thing better than this would be the days before with his father tying his own flies in the peace and serenity of home. That was paradise for Valberg. He could smell his father's grey shirt and watch him create the perfect lure. Parachutes, Salmon Tube, Damsels, Daddies, Sedge Hogs, Nomads and plenty of Executioner Bottle Tube flies. Gustav could make them all, including his own designs: Gustav Wet and Dry, Uppsala Uppers and Malmo Runners. This was joy for Valberg. Not a worry in the world. He could hear his mother humming and singing to herself. Valberg fought hard for those beautiful images. If he had it all back he would never have become a policeman. He would never have let little Patrick's hand go.

'Patrick. Dad. Patrick ...'

'Jon, it's quite alright. Really. Everything is okay.'

Valberg was sitting on the riverbank now with his father having their tea and sandwiches. Everything was fine. Just great. Seamus Heaney and his father read for him together as Valberg held his brother's hand tightly.

Peace at last and finally sleep.

CHAPTER 39

Valberg went into narcoleptic shutdown and slept for the last fifteen hours of his three-day stay in the City Hotel. When he finally awoke he showered and shaved and put on his change of clothes. He ordered room service, tidied the room and left a huge tip. Valberg always tried his best to keep his alcoholism private, but it was not easy. He once had to pay for the entire contents of a hotel mini-fridge that he had consumed on one of his alcoholic binges. He was relieved he did not have to do so this time.

Refreshed and nourished, Valberg made for Strand Road Station on foot. Even though his anger and turmoil had eased to some degree, he still had lingering traces of guilt over Finbar's murder and O'Driscoll's escape.

At the station, Valberg greeted Michael and Linda who were in deep discussion. They returned the greeting warmly. No trip abroad this time, they thought. Valberg knew they were surprised to see him back at work so soon.

'Well, have they found O'Driscoll's body yet?' Valberg asked.

'Nothing yet,' Linda replied. 'But they're still looking.'

'Anything on Sidney Rankin?'

'Nothing there, either,' Michael added. 'We are searching everywhere.'

Linda paused and looked at Valberg. 'Jon. O'Driscoll, you did see him go over the bridge, didn't you?'

'Definitely. He was shot in the side, but he had body protection on so I can't be sure how much it got him. The fall alone would kill a normal person, though.'

'But you did actually see him go over? The Chief says she didn't, she wasn't there with you when the shooting started.'

'There was no-one else on the bridge. What's all this about?'

'Well, Michael and his friend Marty have spent a lot of time looking over all the CCTV stuff we could manage to find and, well ... Here, look at this. Look at the guy with the black-rimmed glasses looking up at our security cameras the other day.'

'What's this?'

Michael ran the footage from four days before, when Dottie Harkin had been at the Strand Road Station looking for Valberg. He played the whole sequence now, strung together, with the heart-rending audio of Dottie Harkin's pleas to the sergeant at the public desk and images of a tall man talking with her on the street outside.

'See here, sir. After he helped her, he looked back and up. There, sir. I'll stop it. The glasses. I recognise those glasses. It's fuzzy, but I'm pretty certain that's the cleaner from the hospital. I got close to him. He does not have a beard here, but I searched him. I'm certain it's him, sir.'

Valberg looked closer. The general size and features looked similar to the man on the bridge. And the way he stood and moved.

Michael told Valberg he and Marty were still working on whatever CCTV material they could salvage from the previous few weeks around where the bodies were found. But so far they had nothing to report.

Valberg found a private room and rang Anna on her personal mobile. He caught her as she was about to go into a meeting with the Policing Board to summarise the recent events in Derry. She stalled them to take the call.

'Wherever you have the Pope, Anna, make sure he's well protected. O'Driscoll is alive. I am sure it's all under control, but you need to protect him and his family.'

'I can't talk now. I'm going in to speak to the policing bores. You're back, then?'

'Lie to them. Don't tell them the truth. Tell them you believe O'Driscoll is dead and the body should be found soon. And yes, I'm back.'

'Thanks, Jon. That's helpful. Jesus, I can't speak at all here. I have to go.'

Linda and Michael pushed open the door just as Valberg was about to make another call.

'They've found a body, Jon,' Linda said. 'It could be him. Right at Boom Hall at the embankment there. It must have been swirling around the river. That's good news, isn't it?'

'Well, let's see who it is first before we say anything. We don't exactly have much to go on from the records, do we?'

'No,' Michael said. 'Everything from the original trial was destroyed. Even his prints. Finbar had been checking all that out and I followed everything up. Even his GP notes. They went to the Health Service Headquarters and can't be found now. He just vanished. Wiped off the face of the earth as if he never existed at all. Do you think he's still playing with us, sir? Torturing us?'

'Who knows? He's an enigma, and a dangerous one at that,' Valberg muttered. 'Let's wait and see what turns up.'

The body found below Boom Hall was that of a fit-looking male between forty-five and fifty of athletic build and just under two metres tall. There were no distinguishing features or any injuries, and death appeared to be from drowning. A post-mortem was to follow as soon as possible. The leaking of that information was enough for the Derry public to believe that Gerard O'Driscoll's body had been found. The news arrived during Anna's explanation to the Policing Board and everyone there was relieved.

The leaks, however, did not take into consideration the clothing the deceased wore or that three days before, a resident of Gransha Hospital had disappeared who matched the dead man's description. He had no identity documents and the hospital had been trying to find out who he was. He had signed himself into the mental institution, claiming he was Satan's son and needed a priest to perform an exorcism. The hospital did not want news of a missing patient revealed. The silence suited everyone while officials tried to figure out who the dead man was.

The media reported that it was 'expected' to be revealed soon that the body found in the River Foyle was that of the serial killer Gerard O'Driscoll.

CHAPTER 40

Valberg broke his own rule and behaved like his father. He became consumed over the following days with the media reporting and analysis of all the events and the ensuing speculation. Calls for a public inquiry into the whole affair intensified, especially in the wake of the revelations of the *Derry Journal* special edition. Draft terms of reference were even mooted so the inquiry could deal with the Force Research Unit, in particular the allegation that a secret unit existed called the Cromwell Killers.

'Just what we need,' Valberg said. 'More lawyers.'

He quickly realised from his new-found passion for the news that every British Government official was petrified at the notion of a public inquiry into the terrible events of the previous month.

The truth is always the first casualty of hostilities, and although the Derry public now felt safer, the bile and anger between politicians, experts and social commentators over who was to blame started. Legal academics weighed in, some calling for reinstating the death penalty, others saying hanging would be too good for the Pope.

'No Pope Here' was dabbed on loyalist and republican walls. All sides agreed at least on that in relation to the shamed ex-chief of the PSNI.

The police and the Public Prosecution Service came under pressure from the British Government to charge the Pope with something, anything that would silence the cries for a public inquiry. Debate in the media increased. The inquiry option was a possibility, not because an inquiry was justified

157

but because the announcement alone would ease the pressure and give government officials time to cover everything up – the way they usually did. The Northern Ireland Executive would have to set up the legalities of any such inquiry as long as the current political situation prevailed, but the go-ahead would come from what Valberg called the 'Mandarin Palace' in Millbank, London – more properly known as the Northern Ireland Office.

As the days went by Valberg watched it all unfold in true Irish compromise style. To fudge the topic and to get television talking about other matters, the Northern Ireland Executive set up a steering group to form a committee to prepare a report on the advisability of an inquiry. The would-be investigation became known as the 'Redacted Inquiry', to be chaired by David McCallum, the 'Invisible Man', as it was clear where it was all going. It would be a private inquiry behind closed doors, everyone anonymous, screened, video-linked from behind a black curtain in a secure location in Tasmania and every document redacted. The judges would be anonymous and the lawyers as well, all in the interests of national security and all in accordance with the Right to Life as enshrined in Article Two of the European Convention on Human Rights. Witnesses, if there were any, would have to agree to discuss nothing publicly on pain of being found in contempt of court and sent to prison.

Public Interest Immunity certificates would fly like confetti at a wedding. By the end of it all, Dottie Harkin would be blamed for sending her innocent daughter out for a pint of milk nearly thirty years ago and for having started everything.

In the meantime, shredders and furnaces became bloated with paper. Journalists were diving for cover. Any person or organisation at risk of being called before an inquiry was busy destroying hard drives and disks of potential evidence. An inquiry could, if run properly, look at hundreds of unresolved murders affecting families whose search for truth and justice had previously been derailed. Even the suggestion of a public inquiry gave those who had a vested interest the chance to destroy what they had and, if necessary, vanish. This was not the justice Dottie Harkin begged for and nearly killed herself over.

Dottie did not know where to turn. Valberg watched her, as it was reported, being forced to stay at home surrounded by photographs of her daughter, one of which she clutched tightly to her chest.

'I just want to know what happened to Orla. I don't want all these solicitors near me. Would someone please tell me what happened to my daughter and why? I don't know what an FRU is or this Mr Cromwell. That doesn't mean anything to me. My wee girl was an angel from heaven. Sent to me by the Lord Jesus Christ and taken from me by the hand of the devil and utter evil. I don't want all these legal things. I'm too old for all that. I tried to put the past behind me. Now it's all back again like a bad smell. Please tell me what happened to my Orla. Someone somewhere knows. I wish no harm to anyone. Please let me die in peace.'

Valberg could see that the media loved her, especially her disdain for the legal profession and the legal process.

But something had to give before the symbolism of the new Peace Bridge opening was filtered around the world and so the fudge of a potential public inquiry was enough to quell the masses. It was delivered sweetly and inevitably.

'So they've nothing to hide, then,' Valberg said to his mother. 'Can you believe it? That poor woman, Mum. What a disgrace. We are all a disgrace. Every one of us.'

'Jon, do you know what I want?'

'What, Mum?'

'I want you to take me to the opening of the Peace Bridge. Would you do that for me? Can we do that together? Just the two of us? I'd like that. Your father would have loved it.'

'Yes, Mum. Of course we will do that. Just me and you.'

Valberg embraced his mother and realised he had not been the son to her that she deserved over the years. She had been left to herself and religion, haunted by the sad memories of Patrick's death. Valberg could not remember the last time she had asked him to do anything. A wave of emotion came over him and a tear came to his eye.

Valberg was glad he had decided to take the new Chief Constable up on her offer of time off work and he took great comfort in helping his mother and staying with her over the next few weeks.

* * *

On Saturday 25 June, Valberg remained true to his word. He got his frail mother as close to the official opening of the Peace Bridge as he could. Thousands turned out to enjoy themselves and even the weather was good.

But Valberg could not entirely switch off. He tensed at the sight of any male over forty-five wearing black thick-rimmed glasses. A few caught his attention but none rang any danger bells. Valberg's mother was talking to some family friends when his mobile rang.

'I thought you were never going to answer. Can you see me, Jon?'

'No, I can't. Show yourself. Where are you?'

'Don't worry, Jon, I'm close. Just dandy, today, ain't it? Just lovely. How are you faring, Jon? Enjoy the City Hotel gig?'

'Where's Rankin? Do you have him? Is he alive?'

'Always on duty, aren't you, Jon? Never fear, Rankin's still with us though he's not crying for his mammy much now. Bloody solicitor. Little Sidney. I'm thinking of letting him go. Can you believe that? And there's me, giving while living or perhaps killing while living. All the same, really. He never made the news much, did he? Says a lot about our dear old respected and esteemed friends in the legal world. What a joke. It was a fair trial.'

'Trial? What do you mean? Where is he?'

'I gave him every opportunity to explain himself. The little wretch. El Sid. Well, I have a full confession from him now. Sir Sidney Rankin. I'm like a Provo nutting squad all on my own, getting everything on tape first. You and yummy Anna are doing okay so far. She's feeding those Police Board morons some merry mendaciousness.'

'Where are you? I'll meet you.'

'Oh, and good luck with the Grimestone trial. Starts next Monday, doesn't it?'

Valberg just grunted. With the recent mayhem and murders, he had forgotten about the approaching court date. He would be there. It was his job and he wanted to support the Whites.

'Or, as lawyers love, another adjournment until the snow is on the ground. Hope the Whites get some justice. Never liked rapists and thieves. Might take a walk up to it, you know, if I get the time. If he's acquitted, just say the word. I'll sort him for you. And yes, I'll let Sid the Solicitor go. Well, it's for the best, isn't it? You know, the mood is so good here today. I was going to go back and disembowel him, but I might save that for Grimestone if he's acquitted. Sid will be home soon. You take care, Jon. There, your mum is looking to go now. Lovely woman. Her friends there are boring her to death almost. And she is so polite. I watched her look after your dad for ages. A great woman. You were very lucky to have a mother and father for so long. You think about that, Jon Valberg. Bye, Jon, for now.'

'Wait. Where are you? Come on, man. Show yourself.'

'Your friends might spot me. Some of my sources in there think we've linked up. But we know that's all nonsense, don't we?'

Valberg remained silent.

'Jon, I think you are under surveillance. There's a shock.'

'I couldn't kill the way you have. Come on. Show yourself. Where are you?'

'Just one more thing. I remember during my time working with the British Army I got word I was off to Belize. Always loved Central America. But then, of course, how bloody stupid of me. I was really part of a killing squad. I learned a lot about kidnapping and killing at close quarters there. It was a good training ground for here. But anyway, the point is, amigo, guess what? That other British colony, Belize, originated from the Maya word *belix*, which sums up everything here well. It means muddy water. We're surrounded by it, Jon, physically and metaphorically, I fear. That's it. Must go ... I think someone has—'

O'Driscoll's phone went dead.

Valberg did not want to ruin the day his mother had looked forward to so much. He looked around and could not be sure but thought he saw O'Driscoll about ten metres away moving rapidly through the crowd. Valberg knew there was security everywhere. If his colleagues were watching, now was the time to move on O'Driscoll and follow him if they could – if those in senior command wanted him captured at all.

'Well, Jon,' Valberg's mother said, 'wasn't that just great? It was everything I expected and more. Of course, there is just one more thing to do and you know what? You just hold my hand and we'll do it now. I don't mind the crowds at all with you beside me. We can walk across the bridge now. Your father and little Patrick can watch us. Here, come this way,' she insisted.

As Valberg walked with his mother over the Peace Bridge towards Ebrington it felt to him like his last act of recovery for now. He realised, however, with O'Driscoll still at large, this was merely the calm before the storm. As he continued on he thought how much his father would have loved this day. For Valberg, even as a policeman, Ebrington was always a place with a sense of mystery. But now the scaffolding and the security fencing were all gone and a space that was hidden away for years and full of secrets was now finally open. He felt cautious but relaxed. However, he could not help thinking about Derry's recent violent sojourn into mayhem; eight murders within days of each other was unprecedented in recent times. At least for now, Valberg thought, the killing was halted.

When they reached the Waterside, Valberg's mother wanted to have a short rest and walk back. The area was saturated with security and media. Surely someone, somewhere would capture an image of O'Driscoll if he were about. Valberg knew that Michael and the others would spend hours hunting through CCTV footage and photographs to see if they could spot anything they could report to him. It was a reassuring thought.

Valberg noticed his mother was a little unsteady. He held her arm as they walked back across the bridge. With luck, soon they could rest up and enjoy the rest of the celebrations.

They had reached the halfway point when Valberg's mobile phone rang again.

CHAPTER 41

'Sorry, Jon, had to hustle there. Thought your people saw me, so I'm a bit out of breath. And the sight of those politicians all smiling for the media and claiming the glory just put me into a downer. I was so close to them I could've ... but maybe another day.'

'Gerry? What's wrong? I thought you were leaving?'

'Jon, once you've learned to kill it's hard to stop.'

'What do you mean, Gerry? What is it?'

'I thought I'd settled the score. But no. I've fallen into the gulf again. There will be more, there has to be more ...'

'Gerry. Take it easy. Talk to me. What's wrong?' Valberg pleaded, desperation in his voice as he looked around him.

'Remember I said I was saving the best for later? On Foyle Bridge? Well here it is. Will I pick twelve at random? Just like a jury? It is my anniversary after all.'

'Gerry. What are you doing? Where are you now?'

'Removing the window and camouflaging my position was harder work than mounting my firing apparatus, custom-made as it is. It's going to be like the siege all over again.'

'The siege?'

'The siege of Sarajevo. Only this time *I* call and make the shots – quite literally in this case. I had to watch then and could do nothing. On the hills a sniper, or a group of them, picked people off. Again at random. I had orders not to interfere.'

'Gerry, whatever you're thinking of doing, don't do it. Don't harm anyone. Please.'

'I had several options to fire from here near the bridge. I scouted all of them and settled on this one. I see you looking. You're looking the wrong way, but then again you're a crafty fellow, Jon. I'm three, maybe four feet in. I thought I'd have bother getting a reference point. A sniper needs one. But look. Spoilt for choice. Bunting and flags everywhere on the bridge.'

'What the bloody hell are you going to do? Stop it.'

'The sky is a bit bruised and sullen. Just like my mood. Keep your voice down and just behave like an idiot on his cell phone. There's always an idiot on a cell phone in the middle of everything.'

'I am calm but worried, Gerry. Worried for my mother and all these innocent people here.'

'Well don't get agitated and give the game away.'

'This is no game.'

'I set this up, Jon, as my grand finale. I have a bead on your head and if I miss I'll hit your mum. It's nice and over-cast and little wind. Perfect.'

'Gerry, don't. Don't.'

'Stop right there, Jon. Give your mother a rest. What about that blonde to your left or the brunette to your right? I'll end all their misery now. One shot. No-one will hear a thing.'

Valberg glanced at the two young women he believed O'Driscoll was referring to.

'Look. I've stopped.'

'I see. I see you clearly through my sight. My finger is on the trigger. One shot to your right upper hemisphere and you are gone. I'm still watching. Listen. You have a rat in the pack. Why is it that at the first sight of politicians and multitudes of police I think of rats? Anyway ... have I got your attention?'

'Go on.'

'You know the answer to every single question I now pose so don't answer. Just listen and think.'

'Right. Go on, I'm listening. You have my attention.'

'Who knew all your movements? Who sent you to Magee on your own? Who knew where your car was parked?

Who stood back and let Finbar get into the car? Who took charge of Finbar's murder scene with Dickey? And why? Think about it. And while you do, think about this, too. Who used to be big buddies with the Pope and was blown off the face of the earth by the Provos? That's right, Jon. Dear old Assistant Chief Constable Rodney Wilson. Linda's father. Just when you think it can't get any darker, it does. She's a naughty girl. Never recovered from her father's murder. And has some unusual friends. Oh, I see you haven't jumped over the bridge. Are you stunned? Is your mind racing?'

'It's hard to take in, Gerry. She is an extremely professional officer. I've never talked to her about her father.'

'The old RUC doesn't want the new PSNI. They don't want Anna that's for sure. Or you. Or perhaps there's another force within a force again? A new one?'

Valberg had visions of a bloodbath developing if he upset O'Driscoll. He imagined bodies falling all around him. In the chaos, O'Driscoll would escape again. Valberg remained calm.

'Gerry, I hear what you say but I cannot accept it.'

'Understood. It is a lot to take in.'

'Why don't you come to me? Talk to me. Please don't harm anyone. Please. Look, there are women and children everywhere. Innocent people.'

O'Driscoll went silent.

'Gerry. Gerry. Are you still there?'

'Anyway, Jon, you're trying hard to talk me out of a massacre, despite the date.'

'What do you mean?'

'It's my anniversary. I told you already. Nearly thirty years ago to this very week. It was a Friday. The trial finished the previous day. The jury came back quick enough. How could I forget? All night sweating. Your dad knew I was innocent. The judge accepted a majority verdict.'

'Jesus, I know, Gerry. Sorry, Gerry. Sorry.'

'Oh, don't you apologise for the sins of others.'

'It was a long time ago, Gerry.'

'What a nasty dictatorship anyway. Time.'

'Gerry, don't harm anyone.'

'My finger is still on the trigger, Jon, so will I pick some targets now at random, start firing, and surround you with dead bodies? Another worldwide advertisement for Derry. Dead bodies on the Peace Bridge. Sure I've nothing to lose. What more can happen to me?'

'No, Gerry. Don't do it. Let's make a deal.'

The line went dead.

By now there was a huge swell of people swarming all around the bridge.

Valberg tensed and fearfully scanned the surrounding area, concentrating on the higher vantage points, waiting for death to come screaming from above. He held his breath. Moments stretched. But nothing came. Relief flooded through him.

Valberg knew where O'Driscoll was. He had spotted some movement high up in a building overlooking the bridge. It had to be him. Valberg quickly thought it through. His phone was being monitored, they would have heard it all. He called Linda to alert her about the contact and direct police to the location.

'I hope I've done the right thing,' Valberg said to his mother who just looked at him blankly.

The PSNI, acting on Valberg's tip-off, descended in huge numbers on the Memorial Hall in Society Street.

No-one noticed Gerard O'Driscoll as he left the City Hotel via the front door and melted into the crowds.